The Woman Who Tried to Be Good

and Other Stories

The Woman Who Tried to Be Good

and Other Stories

EDNA FERBER

WILDSIDE PRESS
Doylestown, Pennsylvania

"Farmer in the Dell" first appeared in print in 1919.

"Long Distance" first appeared in print in 1919.

"That's Marriage" first appeared in print in 1917.

"The Gay Old Dog" first appeared in print in 1917.

"The Maternal Feminine" first appeared in print in 1919.

"The Woman Who Tried to Be Good" first appeared in print in 1913.

"Un Morso doo Pang" first appeared in print in 1919.

The Woman Who Tried to Be Good
and Other Stories
A publication of

WILDSIDE PRESS
P.O. Box 301
Holicong, PA 18928-0301

www.wildsidepress.com

Table of Contents

THE WOMAN WHO TRIED TO BE GOOD 7

THE GAY OLD DOG. 23

THAT'S MARRIAGE 49

FARMER IN THE DELL 79

UN MORSO DOO PANG. 109

LONG DISTANCE 139

THE MATERNAL FEMININE 147

The Woman Who Tried to Be Good

*B*efore she tried to be a good woman she had been a very bad woman — so bad that she could trail her wonderful apparel up and down Main Street, from the Elm Tree Bakery to the railroad tracks, without once having a man doff his hat to her or a woman bow. You passed her on the street with a surreptitious glance, though she was well worth looking at — in her furs and laces and plumes. She had the only full-length mink coat in our town, and Ganz's shoe store sent to Chicago for her shoes. Hers were the miraculously small feet you frequently see in stout women.

Usually she walked alone; but on rare occasions, especially round Christmastime, she might have been seen accompanied by some silent, dull-eyed, stupid-looking girl, who would follow her dumbly in and out of stores, stopping now and then to admire a cheap comb or a chain set with flashy imitation stones — or, queerly enough, a doll with yellow hair and blue eyes and very pink cheeks. But, alone or in company, her appearance in the stores of our town was the signal for a sudden jump in the cost of living. The storekeepers mulcted her; and she knew it and paid in silence, for she was of the class that has no redress. She owned the House with the Closed Shutters, near the freight depot — did Blanche Devine.

In a larger town than ours she would have passed unnoticed. She did not look like a bad woman. Of course she used too much make-up, and as she passed you caught the oversweet breath of a certain heavy scent. Then, too, her diamond eardrops would have made any woman's features look hard; but her plump face, in spite of its heaviness, wore an expression of good-humored intelligence, and her eyeglasses gave her somehow a look of respectability. We do not associate vice with eyeglasses. So in a large city she would have passed for a well-dressed, prosperous, comfortable wife and mother who was in danger of losing her figure from an overabundance of good living; but with us she was a town character, like Old Man Givins, the drunkard, or the weak-minded Binns girl. When she passed the drugstore corner there would be a sniggering among the vacant-eyed loafers idling there, and they would leer at each other and jest in undertones.

So, knowing Blanche Devine as we did, there was something resembling a riot in one of our most respectable neighborhoods when it was learned that she had given up her interest in the house near the freight depot and was going to settle down in the white cottage on the corner and be good. All the husbands in the block, urged on by righteously indignant wives, dropped in on Alderman Mooney after supper to see if the thing could not be stopped. The fourth of the protesting husbands to arrive was the Very Young Husband who lived next door to the corner cottage that Blanche Devine had bought. The Very Young Husband had a Very Young Wife, and they were the joint owners of Snooky. Snooky was three-going-on-four, and looked something like an angel — only healthier and with grimier hands. The whole neighborhood borrowed her and tried to spoil her; but Snooky would not spoil.

Alderman Mooney was down in the cellar, fooling with the furnace.

He was in his furnace overalls; a short black pipe in his mouth. Three protesting husbands had just left. As the Very Young Husband, following Mrs. Mooney's directions, descended the cellar stairs, Alderman Mooney looked up from his tinkering. He peered through a haze of pipe smoke.

"Hello!" he called, and waved the haze away with his open palm.

"Come on down! Been tinkering with this blamed furnace since supper. She don't draw like she ought. 'Long toward spring a furnace always gets balky. How many tons you used this winter?"

"Oh-five," said the Very Young Husband shortly. Alderman Mooney considered it thoughtfully. The Young Husband leaned up against the side of the water tank, his hands in his pockets. "Say, Mooney, is that right about Blanche Devine's having bought the house on the corner?"

"You're the fourth man that's been in to ask me that this evening. I'm expecting the rest of the block before bedtime. She bought it all right."

The Young Husband flushed and kicked at a piece of coal with the toe of his boot.

"Well, it's a darned shame!" he began hotly. "Jen was ready to cry at supper. This'll be a fine neighborhood for Snooky to grow up in! What's a woman like that want to come into a respectable street for, anyway? I own my home and pay my taxes —"

Alderman Mooney looked up.

"So does she," he interrupted. "She's going to improve the place — paint it, and put in a cellar and a furnace, and build a porch, and lay a cement walk all round."

The Young Husband took his hands out of his pockets in order to emphasize his remarks with gestures.

"What's that got to do with it? I don't care if she puts in diamonds for windows and sets out Italian gardens and a terrace with peacocks on it. You're the alderman of this ward, aren't you? Well, it was up to you to keep her out of this block! You could have fixed it with an injunction or something. I'm going to get up a petition — that's what I'm going —"

Alderman Mooney closed the furnace door with a bang that drowned the rest of the threat. He turned the draft in a pipe overhead and brushed his sooty palms briskly together like one who would put an end to a profitless conversation.

"She's bought the house," he said mildly, "and paid for it. And it's hers. She's got a right to live in this neighborhood as long as she acts respectable."

The Very Young Husband laughed.

"She won't last! They never do."

Alderman Mooney had taken his pipe out of his mouth and was rubbing his thumb over the smooth bowl, looking down at it with unseeing eyes. On his face was a queer look — the look of one who is embarrassed because he is about to say something honest.

"Look here! I want to tell you something: I happened to be up in the mayor's office the day Blanche signed for the place. She had to go through a lot of red tape before she got it — had quite a time of it, she did! And say, kid, that woman ain't so — bad."

The Very Young Husband exclaimed impatiently:

"Oh, don't give me any of that, Mooney! Blanche Devine's a town character. Even the kids know what she is. If she's got religion or something, and wants to quit and be decent, why doesn't she go to another town — Chicago or someplace — where nobody knows her?"

That motion of Alderman Mooney's thumb against the smooth pipe bowl stopped. He looked up slowly.

"That's what I said — the mayor too. But Blanche Devine said she wanted to try it here. She said this was home to her. Funny — ain't it? Said she wouldn't be fooling anybody here. They know her. And if she moved away, she said, it'd leak out some way sooner or later. It does, she said. Always! Seems she wants to live like — well, like other women. She put it like this: she says she hasn't got religion, or any of that. She says she's no different than she was when she was twenty. She says that for the last ten years the ambition of her life has been to be able to go into a grocery store and ask the price of, say, celery; and, if the clerk charged her ten when it ought to be seven, to be able to sass him with a regular piece of her mind — and then sail out and trade somewhere else until he saw that she didn't have to stand anything from storekeepers, anymore than any other woman that did her own marketing. She's a smart woman, Blanche is! God knows I ain't taking her part — exactly; but she talked a little, and the mayor and me got a little of her history."

A sneer appeared on the face of the Very Young Husband. He had been known before he met Jen as a rather industrious sower of wild oats. He knew a thing or two, did the Very Young Husband, in spite of his youth! He always fussed when Jen wore even a V-necked summer gown on the street.

"Oh, she wasn't playing for sympathy," went on Alderman Mooney in answer to the sneer. "She said she'd always paid her way and always expected to.

Seems her husband left her without a cent when she was eighteen — with a baby. She worked for four dollars a week in a cheap eating house. The two of 'em couldn't live on that. Then the baby —"

"Good night!" said the Very Young Husband. "I suppose Mrs. Mooney's going to call?"

"Minnie! It was her scolding all through supper that drove me down to monkey with the furnace. She's wild — Minnie is." He peeled off his overalls and hung them on a nail. The Young Husband started to ascend the cellar stairs. Alderman Mooney laid a detaining finger on his sleeve. "Don't say anything in front of Minnie! She's boiling! Minnie and the kids are going to visit her folks out West this summer; so I wouldn't so much as dare to say 'Good morning!' to the Devine woman. Anyway, a person wouldn't talk to her, I suppose. But I kind of thought I'd tell you about her."

"Thanks!" said the Very Young Husband dryly.

In the early spring, before Blanche Devine moved in, there came stone-masons, who began to build something. It was a great stone fireplace that rose in massive incongruity at the side of the little white cottage. Blanche Devine was trying to make a home for herself.

Blanche Devine used to come and watch them now and then as the work progressed. She had a way of walking round and round the house, looking up at it and poking at plaster and paint with her umbrella or fingertip. One day she brought with her a man with a spade. He spaded up a neat square of ground at the side of the cottage and a long ridge near the fence that separated her yard from that of the Very Young Couple next door. The ridge spelled sweet peas and nasturtiums to our small-town eyes.

On the day that Blanche Devine moved in there was wild agitation among the white-ruffed bedroom curtains of the neighborhood. Later on certain odors, as of burning dinners, pervaded the atmosphere. Blanche Devine, flushed and excited, her hair slightly askew, her diamond eardrops flashing, directed the moving, wrapped in her great fur coat; but on the third morning we gasped when she appeared out-of-doors, carrying a little household ladder, a pail of steaming water, and sundry voluminous white cloths. She reared the little ladder against the side of the house, mounted it cautiously, and began to wash windows with housewifely thoroughness. Her stout figure was swathed in a gray sweater and on her head was a battered felt hat — the sort of window — washing costume that has been worn by women from time immemorial. We noticed that she used plenty of hot water and clean rags, and that she rubbed the glass until it sparkled, leaning perilously sideways on the ladder to detect elusive streaks. Our keenest housekeeping eye could find no fault with the way Blanche Devine washed windows.

By May, Blanche Devine had left off her diamond eardrops — perhaps it was their absence that gave her face a new expression. When she went downtown we noticed that her hats were more like the hats the other women in our town wore; but she still affected extravagant footgear, as is right and proper for a stout woman who has cause to be vain of her feet. We noticed that her trips downtown were rare that spring and summer. She used to come home laden with little bundles; and before supper she would change her street clothes for a neat, washable housedress, as is our thrifty custom. Through her bright windows we could see her moving briskly about from kitchen to sitting room; and from the smells that floated out from her kitchen door, she seemed to be preparing for her solitary supper the same homely viands that were frying or stewing or baking in our kitchens. Sometimes you could detect the delectable scent of browning, hot tea biscuit. It takes a determined woman to make tea biscuit for no one but herself.

Blanche Devine joined the church. On the first Sunday morning she came to the service there was a little flurry among the ushers at the vestibule door. They seated her well in the rear. The second Sunday morning a dreadful thing happened. The woman next to whom they seated her turned, regarded her stonily for a moment, then rose agitatedly and moved to a pew across the aisle.

Blanche Devine's face went a dull red beneath her white powder. She never came again — though we saw the minister visit her once or twice. She always accompanied him to the door pleasantly, holding it well open until he was down the little flight of steps and on the sidewalk. The minister's wife did not call.

She rose early, like the rest of us; and as summer came on we used to see her moving about in her little garden patch in the dewy, golden morning. She wore absurd pale-blue negligees that made her stout figure loom immense against the greenery of garden and apple tree. The neighborhood women viewed these negligees with Puritan disapproval as they smoothed down their own prim, starched gingham skirts. They said it was disgusting — and perhaps it was; but the habit of years is not easily overcome. Blanche Devine — snipping her sweet peas, peering anxiously at the Virginia creeper that clung with such fragile fingers to the trellis, watering the flower baskets that hung from her porch — was blissfully unconscious of the disapproving eyes. I wish one of us had just stopped to call good morning to her over the fence, and to say in our neighborly, small-town way: "My, ain't this a scorcher! So early too! It'll be fierce by noon!"

But we did not.

I think perhaps the evenings must have been the

loneliest for her. The summer evenings in our little town are filled with intimate, human, neighborly sounds. After the heat of the day it is pleasant to relax in the cool comfort of the front porch, with the life of the town eddying about us. We sew and read out there until it grows dusk. We call across lots to our next-door neighbor. The men water the lawns and the flower boxes and get together in little, quiet groups to discuss the new street paving. I have even known Mrs. Hines to bring her cherries out there when she had canning to do, and pit them there on the front porch partially shielded by her porch vine, but not so effectually that she was deprived of the sights and sounds about her. The kettle in her lap and the dishpan full of great ripe cherries on the porch floor by her chair, she would pit and chat and peer out through the vines, the red juice staining her plump bare arms.

I have wondered since what Blanche Devine thought of us those lonesome evenings — those evenings filled with friendly sights and sounds. It must have been difficult for her, who had dwelt behind closed shutters so long, to seat herself on the new front porch for all the world to stare at; but she did sit there — resolutely — watching us in silence.

She seized hungrily upon the stray crumbs of conversation that fell to her. The milkman and the iceman and the butcher boy used to hold daily conversation with her. They — sociable gentlemen — would stand on her doorstep, one grimy hand resting against the white of her doorpost, exchanging the time of day with Blanche in the doorway — a tea towel in one hand, perhaps, and a plate in the other. Her little house was a miracle of cleanliness. It was no uncommon sight to see her down on her knees on the kitchen floor, wielding her brush and rag like the rest of us. In canning and preserving time there floated out from her kitchen the pungent scent of pickled crab apples; the mouth-watering smell that meant sweet pickles; or the cloying, divinely sticky odor that meant raspberry jam. Snooky, from her side of the fence, often used to peer through the pickets, gazing in the direction of the enticing smells next door.

Early one September morning there floated out from Blanche Devine's kitchen that fragrant, sweet scent of fresh-baked cookies — cookies with butter in them, and spice, and with nuts on top. Just by the smell of them your mind's eye pictured them coming from the oven-crisp brown circlets, crumbly, delectable. Snooky, in her scarlet sweater and cap, sniffed them from afar and straightway deserted her sand pile to take her stand at the fence. She peered through the restraining bars, standing on tiptoe. Blanche Devine, glancing up from her board and rolling pin, saw the eager golden head. And Snooky, with guile in her heart, raised one fat, dimpled hand above the fence and waved it friendlily. Blanche Devine waved back. Thus encouraged, Snooky's two hands wigwagged frantically above the pickets. Blanche Devine hesitated a moment, her floury hand on her hip. Then she went to the pantry shelf and took out a clean white saucer. She selected from the brown jar on the table three of the brownest, crumbliest, most perfect cookies, with a walnut meat perched atop of each, placed them temptingly on the saucer and, descending the steps, came swiftly across the grass to the triumphant Snooky. Blanche Devine held out the saucer, her lips smiling, her eyes tender. Snooky reached up with one plump white arm.

"Snooky!" shrilled a high voice. "Snooky!" A voice of horror and of wrath. "Come here to me this minute! And don't you dare to touch those!" Snooky hesitated rebelliously, one pink finger in her pouting mouth.

"Snooky! Do you hear me?"

And the Very Young Wife began to descend the steps of her back porch. Snooky, regretful eyes on the toothsome dainties, turned away aggrieved. The Very Young Wife, her lips set, her eyes flashing, advanced and seized the shrieking Snooky by one arm and dragged her away toward home and safety.

Blanche Devine stood there at the fence, holding the saucer in her hand. The saucer tipped slowly, and the three cookies slipped off and fell to the grass. Blanche Devine stood staring at them a moment. Then she turned quickly, went into the house, and shut the door.

It was about this time we noticed that Blanche Devine was away much of the time. The little white cottage would be empty for weeks. We knew she was out of town because the expressman would come for her trunk. We used to lift our eyebrows significantly. The newspapers and handbills would accumulate in a dusty little heap on the porch; but when she returned there was always a grand cleaning, with the windows open, and Blanche — her head bound turbanwise in a towel — appearing at a window every few minutes to shake out a dust cloth. She seemed to put an enormous amount of energy into those cleanings — as if they were a sort of safety valve.

As winter came on she used to sit up before her grate fire long, long after we were asleep in our beds. When she neglected to pull down the shades we could see the flames of her cozy fire dancing gnomelike on the wall. There came a night of sleet and snow, and wind and rattling hail — one of those blustering, wild nights that are followed by morning-paper reports of trains stalled in drifts, mail delayed, telephone and telegraph wires down. It must have been midnight or past when there came a hammering at Blanche Devine's door — a persistent, clamorous rapping. Blanche Devine, sitting before her dying fire half asleep, started and cringed when she heard it, then jumped to her feet, her hand at her breast — her eyes darting this way and that, as though seeking escape.

She had heard a rapping like that before. It had meant bluecoats swarming up the stairway, and frightened cries and pleadings, and wild confusion. So she started forward now, quivering. And then she remembered, being wholly awake now — she remembered, and threw up her head and smiled a little bitterly and walked toward the door. The hammering continued, louder than ever. Blanche Devine flicked on the porch light and opened the door. The half-clad figure of the Very Young Wife next door staggered into the room. She seized Blanche Devine's arm with both her frenzied hands and shook her, the wind and snow beating in upon both of them.

"The baby!" she screamed in a high, hysterical voice. "The baby! The baby — !"

Blanche Devine shut the door and shook the Young Wife smartly by the shoulders.

"Stop screaming," she said quietly. "Is she sick?"

The Young Wife told her, her teeth chattering:

"Come quick! She's dying! Will's out of town. I tried to get the doctor. The telephone wouldn't — I saw your light! For God's sake —"

Blanche Devine grasped the Young Wife's arm, opened the door, and together they sped across the little space that separated the two houses. Blanche Devine was a big woman, but she took the stairs like a girl and found the right bedroom by some miraculous woman instinct. A dreadful choking, rattling sound was coming from Snooky's bed.

"Croup," said Blanche Devine, and began her fight.

It was a good fight. She marshaled her inadequate forces, made up of the half-fainting Young Wife and the terrified and awkward hired girl.

"Get the hot water on — lots of it!" Blanche Devine pinned up her sleeves. "Hot cloths! Tear up a sheet — or anything! Got an oil stove? I want a tea-kettle boiling in the room. She's got to have the steam. If that don't do it we'll raise an umbrella over her and throw a sheet over, and hold the kettle under till the steam gets to her that way. Got any ipecac?"

The Young Wife obeyed orders, white-faced and shaking. Once Blanche Devine glanced up at her sharply.

"Don't you dare faint!" she commanded.

And the fight went on. Gradually the breathing that had been so frightful became softer, easier. Blanche Devine did not relax. It was not until the little figure breathed gently in sleep that Blanche Devine sat back, satisfied. Then she tucked a cover at the side of the bed, took a last satisfied look at the face on the pillow, and turned to look at the wan, disheveled Young Wife.

"She's all right now. We can get the doctor when morning comes — though I don't know's you'll need him."

The Young Wife came round to Blanche Devine's side of the bed and stood looking up at her.

"My baby died," said Blanche Devine simply. The Young Wife gave a little inarticulate cry, put her two hands on Blanche Devine's broad shoulders, and laid her tired head on her breast.

"I guess I'd better be going," said Blanche Devine.

The Young Wife raised her head. Her eyes were round with fright.

"Going! Oh, please stay! I'm so afraid. Suppose she should take sick again! That awful — breathing —"

"I'll stay if you want me to."

"Oh, please! I'll make up your bed and you can rest —"

"I'm not sleepy. I'm not much of a hand to sleep anyway. I'll sit up here in the hall, where there's a light.

You get to bed. I'll watch and see that everything's all right. Have you got something I can read out here — something kind of lively — with a love story in it?"

So the night went by. Snooky slept in her white bed. The Very Young Wife half dozed in her bed, so near the little one. In the hall, her stout figure looming grotesque in wall shadows, sat Blanche Devine, pretending to read. Now and then she rose and tiptoed into the bedroom with miraculous quiet, and stooped over the little bed and listened and looked — and tiptoed away again, satisfied.

The Young Husband came home from his business trip next day with tales of snowdrifts and stalled engines. Blanche Devine breathed a sigh of relief when she saw him from her kitchen window. She watched the house now with a sort of proprietary eye. She wondered about Snooky; but she knew better than to ask. So she waited. The Young Wife next door had told her husband all about that awful night — had told him with tears and sobs. The Very Young Husband had been very, very angry with her — angry, he said, and astonished! Snooky could not have been so sick! Look at her now! As well as ever. And to have called such a woman! Well, he did not want to be harsh; but she must understand that she must never speak to the woman again. Never!

So the next day the Very Young Wife happened to go by with the Young Husband. Blanche Devine spied them from her sitting room window, and she made the excuse of looking in her mailbox in order to go to the door. She stood in the doorway and the Very Young Wife went by on the arm of her husband. She went by — rather white-faced — without a look or a word or a sign!

And then this happened! There came into Blanche Devine's face a look that made slits of her eyes, and drew her mouth down into an ugly, narrow line, and that made the muscles of her jaw tense and hard. It was the ugliest look you can imagine. Then she smiled — if having one's lips curl away from one's teeth can be called smiling.

Two days later there was great news of the white cottage on the corner. The curtains were down; the furniture was packed; the rugs were rolled. The wagons came and backed up to the house and took those things that had made a home for Blanche Devine. And when we heard that she had bought back her interest in the House with the Closed Shutters, near the freight depot, we sniffed.

"I knew she wouldn't last!" we said.

"They never do!" said we.

The Gay Old Dog

*T*hose of you who have dwelt — or even lingered — in Chicago, Illinois, are familiar with the region known as the Loop. For those others of you to whom Chicago is a transfer point between New York and California there is presented this brief explanation:

The Loop is a clamorous, smoke-infested district embraced by the iron arms of the elevated tracks. In a city boasting fewer millions, it would be known familiarly as downtown. From Congress to Lake Street, from Wabash almost to the river, those thunderous tracks make a complete circle, or loop. Within it lie the retail shops, the commercial hotels, the theaters, the restaurants. It is the Fifth Avenue and the Broadway of Chicago.

And he who frequents it by night in search of amusement and cheer is known, vulgarly, as a Loop-hound.

Jo Hertz was a Loop-hound. On the occasion of those sparse first nights granted the metropolis of the Middle West he was always present, third row, aisle, left. When a new Loop café' was opened, Jo's table always commanded an unobstructed view of anything worth viewing. On entering he was wont to say, "Hello,

Gus," with careless cordiality to the headwaiter, the while his eye roved expertly from table to table as he removed his gloves. He ordered things under glass, so that his table, at midnight or thereabouts, resembled a hotbed that favors the bell system. The waiters fought for him. He was the kind of man who mixes his own salad dressing. He liked to call for a bowl, some cracked ice, lemon, garlic, paprika, salt, pepper, vinegar, and oil and make a rite of it. People at near-by tables would lay down their knives and forks to watch, fascinated. The secret of it seemed to lie in using all the oil in sight and calling for more.

That was Jo — a plump and lonely bachelor of fifty. A plethoric, roving-eyed, and kindly man, clutching vainly at the garments of a youth that had long slipped past him. Jo Hertz, in one of those pinch-waist suits and a belted coat and a little green hat, walking up Michigan Avenue of a bright winter's afternoon, trying to take the curb with a jaunty youthfulness against which every one of his fat-encased muscles rebelled, was a sight for mirth or pity, depending on one's vision.

The gay-dog business was a late phase in the life of Jo Hertz. He had been a quite different sort of canine. The staid and harassed brother of three unwed and selfish sisters is an underdog.

At twenty-seven Jo had been the dutiful, hard-working son (in the wholesale harness business) of a widowed and gummidging mother, who called him Joey. Now and then a double wrinkle would appear between Jo's eyes — a wrinkle that had no business there at twenty-seven. Then Jo's mother died, leaving him handicapped by a deathbed promise, the three sisters, and a three-story-and-basement house on Calumet Avenue. Jo's wrinkle became a fixture.

"Joey," his mother had said, in her high, thin voice,

"take care of the girls."

"I will, Ma," Jo had choked.

"Joey," and the voice was weaker, "promise me you won't marry till the girls are all provided for." Then as Jo had hesitated, appalled: "Joey, it's my dying wish. Promise!"

"I promise, Ma," he had said.

Whereupon his mother had died, comfortably, leaving him with a completely ruined life.

They were not bad-looking girls, and they had a certain style, too. That is, Stell and Eva had. Carrie, the middle one, taught school over on the West Side. In those days it took her almost two hours each way. She said the kind of costume she required should have been corrugated steel. But all three knew what was being worn, and they wore it — or fairly faithful copies of it. Eva, the housekeeping sister, had a needle knack. She could skim the State Street windows and come away with a mental photograph of every separate tuck, hem, yoke, and ribbon. Heads of departments showed her the things they kept in drawers, and she went home and reproduced them with the aid of a seamstress by the day. Stell, the youngest, was the beauty. They called her Babe.

Twenty-three years ago one's sisters did not strain at the household leash, nor crave a career. Carrie taught school, and hated it. Eva kept house expertly and complainingly. Babe's profession was being the family beauty, and it took all her spare time. Eva always let her sleep until ten.

This was Jo's household, and he was the nominal head of it. But it was an empty title. The three women dominated his life. They weren't consciously selfish. If you had called them cruel they would have put you down as mad. When you are the lone brother of three sisters, it means that you must constantly be calling for, escorting, or dropping one of them somewhere. Most men of Jo's age were standing before their mirror of a Saturday night, whistling blithely and abstractedly while they discarded a blue polka-dot for a maroon tie, whipped off the maroon for a shot-silk and at the last moment decided against the shot-silk in favor of a plain black-and-white because she had once said she preferred quiet ties. Jo, when he should have been preening his feathers for conquest, was saying:

"Well, my God, I *am* hurrying! Give a man time, can't you? I just got home. You girls been laying around the house all day. No wonder you're ready."

He took a certain pride in seeing his sisters well dressed, at a time when he should have been reveling in fancy waistcoats and brilliant-hued socks, according to the style of that day and the inalienable right of any unwed male under thirty, in any day. On those rare occasions when his business necessitated an out-of-town trip, he would spend half a day floundering about the shops selecting handkerchiefs, or stockings, or feathers, or gloves for the girls. They always turned out to be the wrong kind, judging by their reception.

From Carrie, "What in the world do I want of long white gloves!"

"I thought you didn't have any," Jo would say.

"I haven't. I never wear evening clothes."

Jo would pass a futile hand over the top of his head, as was his way when disturbed. "I just thought you'd like them. I thought every girl liked long white gloves. Just," feebly, "just to — to have."

"Oh, for pity's sake!"

And from Eva or Babe, "I've *got* silk stockings, Jo." Or, "You brought me handkerchiefs the last time."

There was something selfish in his giving, as there always is in any gift freely and joyfully made. They never suspected the exquisite pleasure it gave him to select these things, these fine, soft, silken things. There were many things about this slow-going, amiable brother of theirs that they never suspected. If you had told them he was a dreamer of dreams, for example, they would have been amused. Sometimes, dead-tired by nine o'clock after a hard day downtown, he would doze over the evening paper. At intervals he would wake, red-eyed, to a snatch of conversation such as, "Yes, but if you get a blue you can wear it anywhere. It's dressy, and at the same time it's quiet, too." Eva, the expert, wrestling with Carrie over the problem of the new spring dress. They never guessed that the commonplace man in the frayed old smoking jacket had banished them all from the room long ago; had banished himself, for that matter. In his place was a tall, debonair, and rather dangerously handsome man to whom six o'clock spelled evening clothes. The kind of man who can lean up against a mantel, or propose a toast, or give an order to a manservant, or whisper a gallant speech in a lady's ear with equal ease. The shabby old house on Calumet Avenue was transformed into a brocaded and chandeliered rendezvous for the brilliance of the city. Beauty was here, and wit. But none so beautiful and witty as She. Mrs. — er — Jo Hertz. There was wine, of course; but no vulgar display. There was music; the soft sheen of satin; laughter. And he, the gracious, tactful host, king of his own domain —

"Jo, for heaven's sake, if you're going to snore, go to bed!"

"Why — did I fall asleep?"

"You haven't been doing anything else all evening. A person would think you were fifty instead of thirty."

And Jo Hertz was again just the dull, gray, commonplace brother of three well-meaning sisters.

Babe used to say petulantly, "Jo, why don't you ever

bring home any of your men friends? A girl might as well not have any brother, all the good you do."

Jo, conscience-stricken, did his best to make amends. But a man who has been petticoat-ridden for years loses the knack, somehow, of comradeship with men.

One Sunday in May Jo came home from a late-Sunday-afternoon walk to find company for supper. Carrie often had in one of her schoolteacher friends, or Babe one of her frivolous intimates, or even Eva a staid guest of the old-girl type. There was always a Sunday-night supper of potato salad, and cold meat, and coffee, and perhaps a fresh cake. Jo rather enjoyed it, being a hospitable soul. But he regarded the guests with the undazzled eyes of a man to whom they were just so many petticoats, timid of the night streets and requiring escort home. If you had suggested to him that some of his sisters' popularity was due to his own presence, or if you had hinted that the more kittenish of these visitors were probably making eyes at him, he would have stared in amazement and unbelief.

This Sunday night it turned out to be one of Carrie's friends.

"Emily," said Carrie, "this is my brother, Jo."

Jo had learned what to expect in Carrie's friends. Drab-looking women in the late thirties, whose facial lines all slanted downward.

"Happy to meet you," said Jo, and looked down at a different sort altogether. A most surprisingly different sort, for one of Carrie's friends. This Emily person was very small, and fluffy, and blue-eyed, and crinkly looking. The corners of her mouth when she smiled, and her eyes when she looked up at you, and her hair, which was brown, but had the miraculous effect, somehow, of looking golden.

Jo shook hands with her. Her hand was incredibly small, and soft, so that you were afraid of crushing it, until you discovered she had a firm little grip all her own. It surprised and amused you, that grip, as does a baby's unexpected clutch on your patronizing forefinger. As Jo felt it in his own big clasp, the strangest thing happened to him. Something inside Jo Hertz stopped working for a moment, then lurched sickeningly, then thumped like mad. It was his heart. He stood staring down at her, and she up at him, until the others laughed. Then their hands fell apart, lingeringly.

"Are you a schoolteacher, Emily?" he said.

"Kindergarten. It's my first year. And don't call me Emily, please."

"Why not? It's your name. I think it's the prettiest name in the world." Which he hadn't meant to say at all. In fact, he was perfectly aghast to find himself saying it. But he meant it.

At supper he passed her things, and stared, until everybody laughed again, and Eva said acidly, "Why don't you feed her?"

It wasn't that Emily had an air of helplessness. She just made him feel he wanted her to be helpless, so that he could help her.

Jo took her home, and from that Sunday night he began to strain at the leash. He took his sisters out, dutifully, but he would suggest, with a carelessness that deceived no one, "Don't you want one of your girl friends to come along? That little What's-her-name-Emily, or something. So long's I've got three of you, I might as well have a full squad."

For a long time he didn't know what was the matter with him. He only knew he was miserable, and yet happy. Sometimes his heart seemed to ache with an actual physical ache. He realized that he wanted to do things for Emily. He wanted to buy things for Emily — useless, pretty, expensive things that he couldn't afford.

He wanted to buy everything that Emily needed, and everything that Emily desired. He wanted to marry Emily. That was it. He discovered that one day, with a shock, in the midst of a transaction in the harness business. He stared at the man with whom he was dealing until that startled person grew uncomfortable. "What's the matter, Hertz?" "Matter?" "You look as if you'd seen a ghost or found a gold mine. I don't know which." "Gold mine," said Jo. And then, "No. Ghost." For he remembered that high, thin voice, and his promise. And the harness business was slithering downhill with dreadful rapidity, as the automobile business began its amazing climb. Jo tried to stop it. But he was not that kind of businessman. It never occurred to him to jump out of the down-going vehicle and catch the up-going one. He stayed on, vainly applying brakes that refused to work. "You know, Emily, I couldn't support two households now. Not the way things are. But if you'll wait. If you'll only wait. The girls might — that is, Babe and Carrie —"

She was a sensible little thing, Emily. "Of course I'll wait. But we mustn't just sit back and let the years go by. We've got to help."

She went about it as if she were already a little matchmaking matron. She corralled all the men she had ever known and introduced them to Babe, Carrie, and Eva separately, in pairs, and en masse. She got up picnics. She stayed home while Jo took the three about. When she was present she tried to look as plain and obscure as possible, so that the sisters should show up to advantage. She schemed, and planned, and contrived, and hoped; and smiled into Jo's despairing eyes.

And three years went by. Three precious years. Carrie still taught school, and hated it. Eva kept house more and more complainingly as prices advanced and allowance retreated. Stell was still Babe, the family beauty.

Emily's hair, somehow, lost its glint and began to look just plain brown. Her crinkliness began to iron out.

"Now, look here!" Jo argued, desperately, one night. "We could be happy, anyway. There's plenty of room at the house. Lots of people begin that way. Of course, I couldn't give you all I'd like to, at first. But maybe, after a while —" No dreams of salons, and brocade, and velvet-footed servitors, and satin damask now. Just two rooms, all their own, all alone, and Emily to work for. That was his dream. But it seemed less possible than that other absurd one had been.

Emily was as practical a little thing as she looked fluffy. She knew women. Especially did she know Eva, and Carrie, and Babe. She tried to imagine herself taking the household affairs and the housekeeping pocketbook out of Eva's expert hands. So then she tried to picture herself allowing the reins of Jo's house to remain in Eva's hands. And everything feminine and normal in her rebelled. Emily knew she'd want to put away her own freshly laundered linen, and smooth it, and pat it. She was that kind of woman. She knew she'd want to do her own delightful haggling with butcher and grocer. She knew she'd want to muss Jo's hair, and sit on his knee, and even quarrel with him, if necessary, without the awareness of three ever-present pairs of maiden eyes and ears.

"No! No! We'd only be miserable. I know. Even if they didn't object. And they would, Jo. Wouldn't they?"

His silence was miserable assent. Then, "But you do love me. don't you, Emily?"

"I do, Jo. I love you — and love you — and love you. But, Jo, I — can't."

"I know it, dear. I knew it all the time, really. I just thought, maybe, somehow —"

The two sat staring for a moment into space, their hands clasped.

Then they both shut their eyes with a little shudder, as though what they saw was terrible to look upon. Emily's hand, the tiny hand that was so unexpectedly firm, tightened its hold on his, and his crushed the absurd fingers until she winced with pain.

That was the beginning of the end, and they knew it.

Emily wasn't the kind of girl who would be left to pine. There are too many Jos in the world whose hearts are prone to lurch and then thump at the feel of a soft, fluttering, incredibly small hand in their grip. One year later Emily was married to a young man whose father owned a large, pie-shaped slice of the prosperous state of Michigan.

That being safely accomplished, there was something grimly humorous in the trend taken by affairs in the old house on Calumet. For Eva married. Married well, too, though he was a great deal older than she. She went off in a hat she had copied from a French model at Field's, and a suit she had contrived with a home dressmaker, aided by pressing on the part of the little tailor in the basement over on Thirty-first Street. It was the last of that, though. The next time they saw her, she had on a hat that even she would have despaired of copying, and a suit that sort of melted into your gaze. She moved to the North Side (trust Eva for that), and Babe assumed the management of the household on Calumet Avenue. It was rather a pinched little household now, for the harness business shrank and shrank.

"I don't see how you can expect me to keep house decently on this!" Babe would say contemptuously. Babe's nose, always a little inclined to sharpness, had whittled down to a point of late. "If you knew what Ben gives Eva."

"It's the best I can do, Sis. Business is something

rotten."

"Ben says if you had the least bit of —" Ben was Eva's husband, and quotable, as are all successful men.

"I don't care what Ben says," shouted Jo, goaded into rage. "I'm sick of your everlasting Ben. Go and get a Ben of your own, why don't you, if you're so stuck on the way he does things."

And Babe did. She made a last desperate drive, aided by Eva, and she captured a rather surprised young man in the brokerage way, who had made up his mind not to marry for years and years. Eva wanted to give her her wedding things, but at that Jo broke into sudden rebellion.

"No, sir! No Ben is going to buy my sister's wedding clothes, understand? I guess I'm not broke — yet. I'll furnish the money for her things, and there'll be enough of them, too." Babe had as useless a trousseau, and as filled with extravagant pink-and-blue and lacy and frilly things, as any daughter of doting parents. Jo seemed to find a grim pleasure in providing them. But it left him pretty well pinched. After Babe's marriage (she insisted that they call her Estelle now) Jo sold the house on Calumet. He and Carrie took one of those little flats that were springing up, seemingly overnight, all through Chicago's South Side.

There was nothing domestic about Carrie. She had given up teaching two years before, and had gone into social-service work on the West Side. She had what is known as a legal mind — hard, clear, orderly — and she made a great success of it. Her dream was to live at the Settlement House and give all her time to the work. Upon the little household she bestowed a certain amount of grim, capable attention. It was the same kind of attention she would have given a piece of machinery whose oiling and running had been entrusted to her care. She hated it, and didn't hesitate to say so.

Jo took to prowling about department-store basements, and household goods sections. He was always sending home a bargain in a ham, or a sack of potatoes, or fifty pounds of sugar, or a window clamp, or a new kind of paring knife. He was forever doing odd jobs that the janitor should have done. It was the domestic in him claiming its own.

Then, one night, Carrie came home with a dull glow in her leathery cheeks, and her eyes alight with resolve. They had what she called a plain talk.

"Listen, Jo. They've offered me the job of first assistant resident worker. And I'm going to take it. Take it! I know fifty other girls who'd give their ears for it. I go in next month."

They were at dinner. Jo looked up from his plate, dully. Then he glanced around the little dining room, with its ugly tan walls and its heavy, dark furniture (the Calumet Avenue pieces fitted cumbersomely into the five-room flat).

"Away? Away from here, you mean — to live?"

Carrie laid down her fork. "Well, really, Jo! After all that explanation."

"But to go over there to live! Why, that neighborhood's full of dirt, and disease, and crime, and the Lord knows what all. I can't let you do that, Carrie."

Carrie's chin came up. She laughed a short little laugh. "Let me! That's eighteenth-century talk, Jo. My life's my own to live. I'm going."

And she went.

Jo stayed on in the apartment until the lease was up. Then he sold what furniture he could, stored or gave away the rest, and took a room on Michigan Avenue in one of the old stone mansions whose decayed splendor was being put to such purpose.

Jo Hertz was his own master. Free to marry. Free to

come and go. And he found he didn't even think of marrying. He didn't even want to come or go, particularly. A rather frumpy old bachelor, with thinning hair and a thickening neck.

Every Thursday evening he took dinner at Eva's, and on Sunday noon at Stell's. He tucked his napkin under his chin and openly enjoyed the homemade soup and the well-cooked meats. After dinner he tried to talk business with Eva's husband, or Stell's. His business talks were the old-fashioned kind, beginning:

"Well, now, looka here. Take, f'rinstance, your raw hides and leathers."

But Ben and George didn't want to take, f'rinstance, your raw hides and leathers. They wanted, when they took anything at all, to take golf, or politics, or stocks. They were the modern type of businessman who prefers to leave his work out of his play. Business, with them, was a profession — a finely graded and balanced thing, differing from Jo's clumsy, down-hill style as completely as does the method of a great criminal detective differ from that of a village constable. They would listen, restively, and say, "Uh-uh," at intervals, and at the first chance they would sort of fade out of the room, with a meaning glance at their wives. Eva had two children now. Girls. They treated Uncle Jo with good-natured tolerance. Stell had no children. Uncle Jo degenerated, by almost imperceptible degrees, from the position of honored guest, who is served with white meat, to that of one who is content with a leg and one of those obscure and bony sections which, after much turning with a bewildered and investigating knife and fork, leave one baffled and unsatisfied.

Eva and Stell got together and decided that Jo ought to marry.

"It isn't natural," Eva told him. "I never saw a man who took so little interest in women."

"Me!" protested Jo, almost shyly. "Women!"

"Yes. Of course. You act like a frightened schoolboy."

So they had in for dinner certain friends and acquaintances of fitting age. They spoke of them as "splendid girls." Between thirty-six and forty. They talked awfully well, in a firm, clear way, about civics, and classes, and politics, and economics, and boards. They rather terrified Jo. He didn't understand much that they talked about, and he felt humbly inferior, and yet a little resentful, as if something had passed him by. He escorted them home, dutifully, though they told him not to bother, and they evidently meant it. They seemed capable not only of going home quite unattended but of delivering a pointed lecture to any highwayman or brawler who might molest them.

The following Thursday Eva would say, "How did you like her, Jo?"

"Like who?" Joe would spar feebly.

"Miss Matthews."

"Who's she?"

"Now, don't be funny, Jo. You know very well I mean the girl who was here for dinner. The one who talked so well on the emigration question."

"Oh, her! Why, I liked her all right. Seems to be a smart woman."

"Smart! She's a perfectly splendid girl."

"Sure," Jo would agree cheerfully.

"But didn't you like her?"

"I can't say I did, Eve. And I can't say I didn't. She made me think a lot of a teacher I had in the fifth reader. Name of Himes. As I recall her, she must have been a fine woman. But I never thought of Himes as a woman at all. She was just Teacher."

"You make me tired," snapped Eva impatiently. "A man of your age. You don't expect to marry a girl, do you? A child!"

"I don't expect to marry anybody," Jo had answered.
And that was the truth, lonely though he often was.

The following spring Eva moved to Winnetka. Anyone who got the meaning of the Loop knows the
significance of a move to a North Shore suburb, and
a house. Eva's daughter, Ethel, was growing up, and
her mother had an eye on society.

That did away with Jo's Thursday dinners. Then
Stell's husband bought a car. They went out into the
country every Sunday. Stell said it was getting so that
maids objected to Sunday dinners, anyway. Besides,
they were unhealthful, old-fashioned things. They always meant to ask Jo to come along, but by the time
their friends were placed, and the lunch, and the boxes,
and sweaters, and George's camera, and everything,
there seemed to be no room for a man of Jo's bulk. So
that eliminated the Sunday dinners.

"Just drop in any time during the week," Stell said,
"for dinner. Except Wednesday — that's our bridge
night — and Saturday.

And, of course, Thursday. Cook is out that night.
Don't wait for me to phone."

And so Jo drifted into that sad-eyed, dyspeptic family
made up of those you see dining in second-rate restaurants, their paper propped up against the bowl of
oyster crackers, munching solemnly and with indifference to the stare of the passer-by surveying them
through the brazen plate-glass window.

And then came the war. The war that spelled death
and destruction to millions. The war that brought a
fortune to Jo Hertz, and transformed him, overnight,
from a baggy-kneed old bachelor whose business was
a failure to a prosperous manufacturer whose only
trouble was the shortage in hides for the making of his
product. Leather! The armies of Europe called for it.
Harnesses! More harnesses! Straps! Millions of straps.

More! More!

The musty old harness business over on Lake Street was magically changed from a dust-covered, dead-alive concern to an orderly hive that hummed and glittered with success. Orders poured in. Jo Hertz had inside information on the war. He knew about troops and horses. He talked with French and English and Italian buyers commissioned by their countries to get American-made supplies. And now, when he said to Ben or George, "Take, f'rinstance, your raw hides and leathers," they listened with respectful attention.

And then began the gay-dog business in the life of Jo Hertz. He developed into a Loop-hound, ever keen on the scent of fresh pleasure. That side of Jo Hertz which had been repressed and crushed and ignored began to bloom, unhealthily. At first he spent money on his rather contemptuous nieces. He sent them gorgeous furs, and watch bracelets, and bags. He took two expensive rooms at a downtown hotel, and there was something more tear-compelling than grotesque about the way he gloated over the luxury of a separate ice-water tap in the bathroom. He explained it.

"Just turn it on. Any hour of the day or night. Ice water!"

He bought a car. Naturally. A glittering affair; in color a bright blue, with pale-blue leather straps and a great deal of gold fittings, and special tires. Eva said it was the kind of thing a chorus girl would use, rather than an elderly businessman. You saw him driving about in it, red-faced and rather awkward at the wheel. You saw him, too, in the Pompeian Room at the Congress Hotel of a Saturday afternoon when roving-eyed matrons in mink coats are wont to congregate to sip pale-amber drinks. Actors grew to recognize the semibald head and the shining, round, good-natured face looming out at them from the dim well of the theater, and sometimes, in a musical show, they directed a quip at him, and he liked it. He could pick out the critics as they came down the aisle, and even had a nodding acquaintance with two of them.

"Kelly, of the *Herald,*" he would say carelessly. "Bean, of the *Trib.* They're all afraid of him."

So he frolicked, ponderously. In New York he might have been called a Man About Town.

And he was lonesome. He was very lonesome. So he searched about in his mind and brought from the dim past the memory of the luxuriously furnished establishment of which he used to dream in the evenings when he dozed over his paper in the old house on Calumet. So he rented an apartment, many-roomed and expensive, with a manservant in charge, and furnished it in styles and periods ranging through all the Louis. The living room was mostly rose color. It was like an unhealthy and bloated boudoir. And yet there was nothing sybaritic or uncleanly in the sight of this paunchy, middle-aged man sinking into the rosy-cushioned luxury of his ridiculous home. It was a frank and naïve indulgence of long-starved senses, and there was in it a great resemblance to the rolling-eyed ecstasy of a schoolboy smacking his lips over an all-day sucker.

The war went on, and on, and on. And the money continued to roll in — a flood of it. Then, one afternoon, Eva, in town on shopping bent, entered a small, exclusive, and expensive shop on Michigan Avenue. Eva's weakness was hats. She was seeking a hat now. She described what she sought with a languid conciseness, and stood looking about her after the saleswoman had vanished in quest of it. The room was becomingly rose-illumined and somewhat dim, so that some minutes had passed before she realized that a man seated on a raspberry brocade settee not five feet away — a man with a walking stick, and yellow gloves, and tan spats, and a check suit — was her brother Jo. From him Eva's wild-eyed glance leaped to the woman who was trying on hats before one of the many long mirrors. She was seated, and a saleswoman was exclaiming discreetly at her elbow.

Eva turned sharply and encountered her own saleswoman returning hat-laden. "Not today," she gasped. "I'm feeling ill. Suddenly." And almost ran from the room.

That evening she told Stell, relating her news in that telephone pidgin English devised by every family of married sisters as protection against the neighbors. Translated, it ran thus:

"He looked straight at me. My dear, I thought I'd die! But at least he had sense enough not to speak. She was one of those limp, willowy creatures with the greediest eyes that she tried to keep softened to a baby stare, and couldn't, she was so crazy to get her hands on those hats. I saw it all in one awful minute. You know the way I do. I suppose some people would call her pretty. I don't. And her color. Well! And the most expensive-looking hats. Not one of them under seventy-five. Isn't it disgusting! At his age! Suppose Ethel had been with me!"

The next time it was Stell who saw them. In a restaurant. She said it spoiled her evening. And the third time it was Ethel. She was one of the guests at a theater party given by Nicky Overton II. The North Shore Overtons. Lake Forest. They came in late, and occupied the entire third row at the opening performance of Believe Me! And Ethel was Nicky's partner. She was glowing like a rose. When the lights went up after the first act Ethel saw that her uncle Jo was seated just ahead of her with what she afterward described as a blonde. Then her uncle had turned around, and seeing her, had been surprised into a smile that spread genially all over his plump and rubicund face. Then he had turned to face forward again, quickly.

"Who's the old bird?" Nicky had asked. Ethel had pretended not to hear, so he had asked again.

"My uncle," Ethel answered, and flushed all over her delicate face, and down to her throat. Nicky had looked at the blonde, and his eyebrows had gone up ever so slightly.

It spoiled Ethel's evening. More than that, as she told her mother of it later, weeping, she declared it had spoiled her life.

Eva talked it over with her husband in that intimate hour that precedes bedtime. She gesticulated heatedly with her hairbrush.

"It's disgusting, that's what it is. Perfectly disgusting. There's no fool like an old fool. Imagine! A creature like that. At his time of life."

"Well, I don't know," Ben said, and even grinned a little. "I suppose a boy's got to sow his wild oats sometime."

"Don't be anymore vulgar than you can help," Eva retorted. "And I think you know, as well as I, what it means to have that Overton boy interested in Ethel."

"If he's interested in her," Ben blundered, "I guess the fact that Ethel's uncle went to the theater with someone who isn't Ethel's aunt won't cause a shudder to run up and down his frail young frame, will it?"

"All right," Eva had retorted. "If you're not man enough to stop it, I'll have to, that's all. I'm going up there with Stell this week."

They did not notify Jo of their coming. Eva telephoned his apartment when she knew he would be out, and asked his man if he expected his master home to dinner that evening. The man had said yes. Eva arranged to meet Stell in town. They would drive to Jo's apartment together, and wait for him there.

When she reached the city Eva found turmoil there. The first of the American troops to be sent to France were leaving. Michigan Boulevard was a billowing, surging mass: flags, pennants, banners, crowds. All the elements that make for demonstration. And over the whole-quiet. No holiday crowd, this. A solid, determined mass of people waiting patient hours to see the khaki-clads go by. Three years had brought them to a clear knowledge of what these boys were going to.

"Isn't it dreadful!" Stell gasped.

"Nicky Overton's too young, thank goodness."

Their car was caught in the jam. When they moved at all, it was by inches. When at last they reached Jo's apartment they were flushed, nervous, apprehensive. But he had not yet come in. So they waited.

No, they were not staying to dinner with their brother, they told the relieved houseman.

Stell and Eva, sunk in rose-colored cushions, viewed the place with disgust and some mirth. They rather avoided each other's eyes.

"Carrie ought to be here," Eva said. They both smiled at the thought of the austere Carrie in the midst of those rosy cushions, and hangings, and lamps. Stell rose and began to walk about restlessly. She picked up a vase and laid it down; straightened a picture. Eva got up, too, and wandered into the hall. She stood there a moment, listening. Then she turned and passed into Jo's bedroom, Stell following. And there you knew Jo for what he was.

This room was as bare as the other had been ornate. It was Jo, the clean-minded and simple-hearted, in revolt against the cloying luxury with which he had surrounded himself. The bedroom, of all rooms in any house, reflects the personality of its occupant. True, the actual furniture was paneled, cupid-surmounted, and ridiculous. It had been the fruit of Jo's first orgy of the senses. But now it stood out in that stark little room with an air as incongruous and ashamed as that of a pink tarlatan danseuse who finds herself in a monk's cell. None of those wall pictures with which bachelor bedrooms are reputed to be hung. No satin slippers. No scented notes. Two plain-backed military brushes on the chiffonier (and he so nearly hairless!). A little orderly stack of books on the table near the bed. Eva fingered their titles and gave a little gasp. One of them was on gardening.

"Well, of all things!" exclaimed Stell. A book on the war, by an Englishman. A detective story of the lurid type that lulls us to sleep. His shoes ranged in a careful row in the closet, with a shoe tree in every one of them. There was something speaking about them. They looked so human. Eva shut the door on them quickly. Some bottles on the dresser. A jar of pomade. An ointment such as a man uses who is growing bald and is panic-stricken too late. An insurance calendar on the wall. Some rhubarb-and-soda mixture on the shelf in the bathroom, and a little box of pepsin tablets.

"Eats all kinds of things at all hours of the night," Eva said, and wandered out into the rose-colored front room again with the air of one who is chagrined at her failure to find what she has sought. Stell followed her furtively.

"Where do you suppose he can be?" she demanded. "It's" — she glanced at her wrist — "why, it's after six!"

And then there was a little click. The two women sat up, tense. The door opened. Jo came in. He blinked a little. The two women in the rosy room stood up.

"Why — Eve! Why, Babe! Well! Why didn't you let me know?"

"We were just about to leave. We thought you weren't coming home."

Jo came in slowly.

"I was in the jam on Michigan, watching the boys go by." He sat down, heavily. The light from the window fell on him. And you saw that his eyes were red.

He had found himself one of the thousands in the jam on Michigan Avenue, as he said. He had a place near the curb, where his big frame shut off the view of the unfortunates behind him. He waited with the placid interest of one who has subscribed to all the funds and societies to which a prosperous, middle-aged businessman is called upon to subscribe in war-time. Then, just as he was about to leave, impatient at the delay, the crowd had cried, with a queer, dramatic, exultant note in its voice, "Here they come! Here come the boys!"

Just at that moment two little, futile, frenzied fists began to beat a mad tattoo on Jo Hertz's broad back. Jo tried to turn in the crowd, all indignant resentment. "Say, looka here!"

The little fists kept up their frantic beating and pushing. And a voice — a choked, high little voice — cried, "Let me by! I can't see! You *man*, you! You big fat man! My boy's going by — to war — and I can't see! Let me by!"

Jo scrooged around, still keeping his place. He looked down. And upturned to him in agonized appeal was the face of Emily. They stared at each other for what seemed a long, long time. It was really only the fraction of a second. Then Jo put one great arm firmly around Emily's waist and swung her around in front of him. His great bulk protected her. Emily was clinging to his hand. She was breathing rapidly, as if she had been running. Her eyes were straining up the street.

"Why, Emily, how in the world — !"

"I ran away. Fred didn't want me to come. He said it would excite me too much."

"Fred?"

"My husband. He made me promise to say good-bye to Jo at home."

"Jo?"

"Jo's my boy. And he's going to war. So I ran away. I had to see him. I had to see him go."

She was dry-eyed. Her gaze was straining up the street.

"Why, sure," said Jo. "Of course you want to see him." And then the crowd gave a great roar. There came over Jo a feeling of weakness. He was trembling. The boys went marching by.

"There he is," Emily shrilled, above the din. "There he is! There he is! There he —" And waved a futile little hand. It wasn't so much a wave as a clutching. A clutching after something beyond her reach.

"Which one? Which one, Emily?"

"The handsome one. The handsome one." Her voice quavered and died.

Jo put a steady hand on her shoulder. "Point him out," he commanded "Show me." And the next instant, "Never mind. I see him."

Somehow, miraculously, he had picked him from among the hundreds. Had picked him as surely as his own father might have. It was Emily's boy. He was marching by, rather stiffly. He was nineteen, and fun-loving, and he had a girl, and he didn't particularly want to go to France and — to go to France. But more than he had hated going, he had hated not to go. So he marched by, looking straight ahead, his jaw set so that his chin stuck out just a little. Emily's boy.

Jo looked at him, and his face flushed purple. His eyes, the hard-boiled eyes of a Loop-hound, took on the look of a sad old man. And suddenly he was no longer Jo, the sport; old J. Hertz, the gay dog. He was Jo Hertz, thirty, in love with life, in love with Emily,

and with the stinging blood of young manhood cours-
ing through his veins.

Another minute and the boy had passed on up the
broad street — the fine, flag-bedecked street — just one
of a hundred service hats bobbing in rhythmic motion
like sandy waves lapping a shore and flowing on.

Then he disappeared altogether.

Emily was clinging to Jo. She was mumbling something, over and over. "I can't. I can't. Don't ask me to.
I can't let him go.

Like that. I can't."

Jo said a queer thing.

"Why, Emily! We wouldn't have him stay home,
would we? We wouldn't want him to do anything
different, would we? Not our boy. I'm glad he enlisted.
I'm proud of him. So are you glad."

Little by little he quieted her. He took her to the car
that was waiting, a worried chauffeur in charge. They
said good-bye, awkwardly. Emily's face was a red, swol-
len mass.

So it was that when Jo entered his own hallway half
an hour later he blinked, dazedly, and when the light
from the window fell on him you saw that his eyes were
red.

Eva was not one to beat about the bush. She sat
forward in her chair, clutching her bag rather nervously.

"Now, look here, Jo. Stell and I are here for a reason.
We're here to tell you that this thing's going to stop."

"Thing? Stop?"

"You know very well what I mean. You saw me at the
milliner's that day. And night before last, Ethel. We're
all disgusted. If you must go about with people like
that, please have some sense of decency."

Something gathering in Jo's face should have warned
her. But he was slumped down in his chair in such a

huddle, and he looked so old and fat that she did not heed it. She went on. "You've got us to consider. Your sisters. And your nieces. Not to speak of your own —"

But he got to his feet then, shaking, and at what she saw in his face even Eva faltered and stopped. It wasn't at all the face of a fat, middle-aged sport. It was a face Jovian, terrible.

"You!" he began, low-voiced, ominous. "You!" He raised a great fist high. "You two murderers! You didn't consider me, twenty years ago. You come to me with talk like that. Where's my boy! You killed him, you two, twenty years ago. And now he belongs to some-body else. Where's my son that should have gone marching by today?" He flung his arms out in a great gesture of longing. The red veins stood out on his forehead. "Where's my son! Answer me that, you two selfish, miserable women. Where's my son!" Then, as they huddled together, frightened, wild-eyed.

"Out of my house! Out of my house! Before I hurt you!"

They fled, terrified. The door banged behind them.

Jo stood, shaking, in the center of the room. Then he reached for a chair, gropingly, and sat down. He passed one moist, flabby hand over his forehead and it came away wet. The telephone rang. He sat still. It sounded far away and unimportant, like something forgotten. But it rang and rang insistently. Jo liked to answer his telephone when he was at home.

"Hello!" He knew instantly the voice at the other end.

"That you, Jo?" it said.

"Yes."

"How's my boy?"

"I'm — all right."

"Listen, Jo. The crowd's coming over tonight. I've fixed up a little poker game for you. Just eight of us."

"I can't come tonight, Gert."

"Can't! Why not?"

"I'm not feeling so good."

"You just said you were all right."

"I *am* all right. Just kind of tired."

The voice took on a cooing note. "Is my Joey tired? Then he shall be all comfy on the sofa, and he doesn't need to play if he don't want to. No, sir."

Jo stood staring at the black mouthpiece of the telephone. He was seeing a procession go marching by. Boys, hundreds of boys, in khaki.

"Hello! Hello!" The voice took on an anxious note. "Are you there?"

"Yes," wearily.

"Jo, there's something the matter. You're sick. I'm coming right over."

"No!" "Why not? You sound as if you'd been sleeping. Look here —"

"Leave me alone!" cried Jo, suddenly, and the receiver clacked onto the hook. "Leave me alone. Leave me alone." Long after the connection had been broken.

He stood staring at the instrument with unseeing eyes. Then he turned and walked into the front room. All the light had gone out of it. Dusk had come on. All the light had gone out of everything. The zest had gone out of life. The game was over — the game he had been playing against loneliness and disappointment. And he was just a tired old man. A lonely, tired old man in a ridiculous rose-colored room that had grown, all of a sudden, drab {sic}

That's Marriage

*T*heresa Platt (she had been Terry Sheehan) watched her husband across the breakfast table with eyes that smoldered. But Orville Platt was quite unaware of any smoldering in progress. He was occupied with his eggs. How could he know that these very eggs were feeding the dull red menace in Terry Platt's eyes?

When Orville Platt ate a soft-boiled egg he concentrated on it. He treated it as a great adventure. Which, after all, it is. Few adjuncts of our daily life contain the element of chance that is to be found in a three-minute breakfast egg.

This was Orville Platt's method of attack: first, he chipped off the top, neatly. Then he bent forward and subjected it to a passionate and relentless scrutiny. Straightening — preparatory to plunging his spoon therein — he flapped his right elbow. It wasn't exactly a flap; it was a pass between a hitch and a flap, and presented external evidence of a mental state. Orville Platt always gave that little preliminary jerk when he was contemplating a serious step, or when he was moved, or argumentative. It was a trick as innocent as it was maddening.

Terry Platt had learned to look for that flap — they had been married four years — to look for it, and to hate it with a morbid, unreasoning hate. That flap of the elbow was tearing Terry Platt's nerves into raw, bleeding fragments.

Her fingers were clenched tightly under the table, now. She was breathing unevenly. "If he does that again," she told herself, "if he flaps again when he opens the second egg, I'll scream. I'll scream. I'll scream! I'll sc —"

He had scooped the first egg into his cup. Now he picked up the second, chipped it, concentrated, straightened, then — up went the elbow, and down, with the accustomed little flap.

The tortured nerves snapped. Through the early-morning quiet of Wetona, Wisconsin, hurtled the shrill, piercing shriek of Terry Platt's hysteria.

"Terry! For God's sake! What's the matter!"

Orville Platt dropped the second egg, and his spoon. The egg yolk trickled down his plate. The spoon made a clatter and flung a gay spot of yellow on the cloth. He started toward her.

Terry, wild-eyed, pointed a shaking finger at him. She was laughing, now, uncontrollably. "Your elbow! Your elbow!"

"Elbow?" He looked down at it, bewildered, then up, fright in his face. "What's the matter with it?"

She mopped her eyes. Sobs shook her. "You f-f-flapped it."

"F-f-f —" The bewilderment in Orville Platt's face gave way to anger. "Do you mean to tell me that you screeched like that because my — because I moved my elbow?"

"Yes."

His anger deepened and reddened to fury. He choked. He had started from his chair with his napkin in his hand. He still clutched it. Now he crumpled it into a wad and hurled it to the center of the table, where it struck a sugar bowl, dropped back, and uncrumpled slowly, reprovingly. "You — you —" Then bewilderment closed down again like a fog over his countenance. "But why? I can't see —"

"Because it — because I can't stand it any longer. Flapping. This is what you do. Like this."

And she did it. Did it with insulting fidelity, being a clever mimic.

"Well, all I can say is you're crazy, yelling like that, for nothing."

"It isn't nothing."

"Isn't, huh? If that isn't nothing, what is?" They were growing incoherent. "What d'you mean, screeching like a maniac?

Like a wild woman? The neighbors'll think I've killed you. What d'you mean, anyway!"

"I mean I'm tired of watching it, that's what. Sick and tired."

"Y'are, huh? Well, young lady, just let me tell *you* something —"

He told her. There followed one of those incredible quarrels, as sickening as they are human, which can take place only between two people who love each other; who love each other so well that each knows with cruel certainty the surest way to wound the other; and who stab, and tear, and claw at these vulnerable spots in exact proportion to their love.

Ugly words. Bitter words. Words that neither knew they knew flew between them like sparks between steel striking steel.

From him: "Trouble with you is you haven't got enough to do. That's the trouble with half you women. Just lay around the house, rotting. I'm a fool, slaving on the road to keep a good-for-nothing —"

"I suppose you call sitting around hotel lobbies slaving! I suppose the house runs itself! How about my evenings? Sitting here alone, night after night, when you're on the road."

Finally, "Well, if you don't like it," he snarled, and lifted his chair by the back and slammed it down, savagely, "if you don't like it, why don't you get out, hm? Why don't you get out?"

And from her, her eyes narrowed to two slits, her cheeks scarlet:

"Why, thanks. I guess I will."

Ten minutes later he had flung out of the house to catch the 8:19 for Manitowoc. He marched down the street, his shoulders swinging rhythmically to the weight of the burden he carried — his black leather handbag and the shiny tan sample case, battle-scarred, both, from many encounters with ruthless porters and busmen and bellboys. For four years, as he left for his semi-monthly trip, he and Terry had observed a certain little ceremony (as had the neighbors). She would stand in the doorway, watching him down the street, the heavier sample case banging occasionally at his shin. The depot was only three blocks away. Terry watched him with fond but unillusioned eyes, which proves that she really loved him. He was a dapper, well-dressed fat man, with a weakness for pronounced patterns in suitings, and addicted to derbies. One week on the road, one week at home. That was his routine. The wholesale grocery trade liked Platt, and he had for his customers the fondness that a traveling salesman has who is successful in his territory. Before his marriage to Terry Sheehan his little red address book had been overwhelming proof against the theory that nobody loves a fat man.

Terry, standing in the doorway, always knew that when he reached the corner just where Schroeder's house threatened to hide him from view, he would stop, drop the sample case, wave his hand just once, pick up the sample case and go on, proceeding backward for a step or two until Schroeder's house made good its threat. It was a comic scene in the eyes of the onlooker, perhaps because a chubby Romeo offends the sense of fitness. The neighbors, lurking behind their parlor curtains, had laughed at first. But after a while they learned to look for that little scene, and to take it unto themselves, as if it were a personal thing. Fifteen-year wives whose husbands had long since abandoned flowery farewells used to get a vicarious thrill out of it, and to eye Terry with a sort of envy.

This morning Orville Platt did not even falter when he reached Schroeder's corner. He marched straight on, looking steadily ahead, the heavy bags swinging from either hand. Even if he had stopped — though she knew he wouldn't — Terry Platt would not have seen him. She remained seated at the disordered breakfast table, a dreadfully still figure, and sinister; a figure of stone and fire, of ice and flame. Over and over in her mind she was milling the things she might have said to him, and had not. She brewed a hundred vitriolic cruelties that she might have flung in his face. She would concoct one biting brutality, and dismiss it for a second, and abandon that for a third. She was too angry to cry — a dangerous state in a woman. She was what is known as cold mad, so that her mind was working clearly and with amazing swiftness, and yet as though it were a thing detached; a thing that was no part of her.

She sat thus for the better part of an hour, motionless except for one forefinger that was, quite unconsciously, tapping out a popular and cheap little air that she had been strumming at the piano the evening before, having bought it downtown that same afternoon. It had struck Orville's fancy, and she had played it over and over for him. Her right forefinger was playing the entire tune, and something in the back of her head was following it accurately, though the separate thinking process was going on just the same. Her eyes were bright, and wide, and hot. Suddenly she became conscious of the musical antics of her finger. She folded it in with its mates, so that her hand became a fist. She stood up and stared down at the clutter of the breakfast table. The egg — that fateful second egg — had congealed to a mottled mess of yellow and white. The spoon lay on the cloth. His coffee, only half consumed, showed tan with a cold gray film over it. A slice of toast at the left of his plate seemed to grin at her with the semi-circular wedge that he had bitten out of it.

Terry stared down at these congealing remnants. Then she laughed, a hard high little laugh, pushed a plate away contemptuously with her hand, and walked into the sitting room. On the piano was the piece of music (Bennie Gottschalk's great song hit, "Hicky Boola") which she had been playing the night before. She picked it up, tore it straight across, once, placed the pieces back to back, and tore it across again. Then she dropped the pieces to the floor.

"You bet I'm going," she said, as though concluding a train of thought. "You just bet I'm going. Right now!" And Terry went. She went for much the same reason as that given by the ladye of high degree in the old English song — she who had left her lord and bed and board to go with the raggle-taggle gypsies-O! The thing that was sending Terry Platt away was much more than a conjugal quarrel precipitated by a soft-boiled egg and a flap of the arm. It went so deep that it is necessary to delve back to the days when Theresa Platt was Terry Sheehan to get the real significance of it, and of the things she did after she went.

When Mrs. Orville Platt had been Terry Sheehan, she
had played the piano, afternoons and evenings, in the
orchestra of the Bijou Theater, on Cass Street, Wetona,
Wisconsin. Anyone with a name like Terry Sheehan
would, perforce, do well anything she might set out to
do. There was nothing of genius in Terry, but there was
something of fire, and much that was Irish. Which
meant that the Watson Team, Eccentric Song and
Dance Artists, never needed a rehearsal when they
played the Bijou. Ruby Watson used merely to ap-
proach Terry before the Monday performance, sheet
music in hand, and say, "Listen, dearie. We've got some
new business I want to wise you to. Right here it goes
'*Tum* dee-dee *dum* dee-dee *tum dum dum*.' See? Like that.
And then Jim vamps. Get me?"

Terry, at the piano, would pucker her pretty brow a
moment. Then, "Like this, you mean?"

"That's it! You've got it."

"All right. I'll tell the drum."

She could play any tune by ear, once heard. She got
the spirit of a thing, and transmitted it. When Terry
played a martial number you tapped the floor with
your foot, and unconsciously straightened your shoulders. When she played a home-and-mother song you
hoped that the man next to you didn't know you were
crying (which he probably didn't, because he was weeping, too).

At that time motion pictures had not attained their
present virulence. Vaudeville, polite or otherwise, had
not yet been crowded out by the ubiquitous film. The
Bijou offered entertainment of the cigar-box-tramp
variety, interspersed with trick bicyclists, soubrettes in
slightly soiled pink, trained seals, and Family Fours
with lumpy legs who tossed each other about and
struck Goldbergian attitudes.

Contact with these gave Terry Sheehan a semiprofessional tone. The more conservative of her townspeople looked at her askance. There never had been an evil thing about Terry, but Wetona considered her rather fly. Terry's hair was very black, and she had a fondness for those little, close-fitting scarlet turbans. Terry's mother had died when the girl was eight, and Terry's father had been what is known as easygoing. A good-natured, lovable, shiftless chap in the contracting business. He drove around Wetona in a sagging, one-seated cart and never made any money because he did honest work and charged as little for it as men who did not. His mortar stuck, and his bricks did not crumble, and his lumber did not crack. Riches are not acquired in the contracting business in that way. Ed Sheehan and his daughter were great friends. When he died (she was nineteen) they say she screamed once, like a banshee, and dropped to the floor.

After they had straightened out the muddle of books in Ed Sheehan's gritty, dusty little office Terry turned her piano-playing talent to practical account. At twenty-one she was still playing at the Bijou, and into her face was creeping the first hint of that look of sophistication which comes from daily contact with the artificial world of the footlights.

There are, in a small Midwest town like Wetona, just two kinds of girls. Those who go downtown Saturday nights, and those who don't. Terry, if she had not been busy with her job at the Bijou, would have come in the first group. She craved excitement. There was little chance to satisfy such craving in Wetona, but she managed to find certain means. The traveling men from the Burke House just across the street used to drop in at the Bijou for an evening's entertainment. They usually sat well toward the front, and Terry's expert playing, and the gloss of her black hair, and her piquant profile as she sometimes looked up toward the stage for a signal from one of the performers caught their fancy, and held it.

She found herself, at the end of a year or two, with a rather large acquaintance among these peripatetic gentlemen. You occasionally saw one of them strolling home with her. Sometimes she went driving with one of them of a Sunday afternoon. And she rather enjoyed taking Sunday dinner at the Burke Hotel with a favored friend. She thought those small-town hotel Sunday dinners the last word in elegance. The roast course was always accompanied by an aqueous, semifrozen concoction which the bill of fare revealed as Roman Punch. It added a royal touch to the repast, even when served with roast pork.

Terry was twenty-two when Orville Platt, making his initial Wisconsin trip for the wholesale grocery house he represented, first beheld her piquant Irish profile, and heard her deft manipulation of the keys. Orville had the fat man's sense of rhythm and love of music. He had a buttery tenor voice, too, of which he was rather proud.

He spent three days in Wetona that first trip, and every evening saw him at the Bijou, first row, center. He stayed through two shows each time, and before he had been there fifteen minutes Terry was conscious of him through the back of her head. Orville Platt paid no more heed to the stage, and what was occurring thereon, than if it had not been. He sat looking at Terry, and waggling his head in time to the music. Not that Terry was a beauty. But she was one of those immaculately clean types. That look of fragrant cleanliness was her chief charm. Her clear, smooth skin contributed to it, and the natural penciling of her eyebrows. But the thing that accented it, and gave it a last touch, was the way in which her black hair came down in a little point just in the center of her forehead, where hair meets brow. It grew to form what is known as a cowlick. (A prettier name for it is widow's peak.) Your eye lighted on it, pleased, and from it traveled its gratified way down her white temples, past her little ears, to the smooth black coil at the nape of her neck. It was a trip that rested you.

At the end of the last performance on the night of his second visit to the Bijou, Orville waited until the audience had begun to file out. Then he leaned forward over the rail that separated orchestra from audience.

"Could you," he said, his tones dulcet, "could you oblige me with the name of that last piece you played?"

Terry was stacking her music. "George!" she called to the drum. "Gentleman wants to know the name of that last piece." And prepared to leave.

"'My Georgia Crackerjack,'" said the laconic drum.

Orville Platt took a hasty side step in the direction of the door toward which Terry was headed. "It's a pretty thing," he said fervently. "An awful pretty thing. Thanks. It's beautiful."

Terry flung a last insult at him over her shoulder: "Don't thank *me* for it. I didn't write it."

Orville Platt did not go across the street to the hotel. He wandered up Cass Street, and into the ten-o'clock quiet of Main Street, and down as far as the park and back. "Pretty as a pink! And play! . . . And good, too. Good."

A fat man in love.

At the end of six months they were married. Terry was surprised into it. Not that she was not fond of him. She was; and grateful to him, as well. For, pretty as she was, no man had ever before asked Terry to be his wife. They had made love to her. They had paid court to her. They had sent her large boxes of stale drugstore chocolates, and called her endearing names as they made cautious declarations such as:

"I've known a lot of girls, but you've got something different. I don't know. You've got so much sense. A fellow can chum around with you. Little pal."

Wetona would be their home. They rented a comfortable, seven-room house in a comfortable, middle-class neighborhood, and Terry dropped the red velvet turbans and went in for picture hats. Orville bought her a piano whose tone was so good that to her ear, accustomed to the metallic discords of the Bijou instrument, it sounded out of tune. She played a great deal at first, but unconsciously she missed the sharp spat of applause that used to follow her public performance. She would play a piece, brilliantly, and then her hands would drop to her lap. And the silence of her own sitting room would fall flat on her ears. It was better on the evenings when Orville was home. He sang, in his throaty, fat man's tenor, to Terry's expert accompaniment.

"This is better than playing for those ham actors, isn't it, hon?" And he would pinch her ear.

"Sure" — listlessly.

But after the first year she became accustomed to what she termed private life. She joined an afternoon sewing club, and was active in the ladies' branch of the U.C.T. She developed a knack at cooking, too, and Orville, after a week or ten days of hotel fare in small Wisconsin towns, would come home to sea-foam biscuits, and real soup, and honest pies and cake. Sometimes, in the midst of an appetizing meal he would lay down his knife and fork and lean back in his chair, and regard the cool and unruffled Terry with a sort of reverence in his eyes. Then he would get up, and come around to the other side of the table, and tip her pretty face up to his.

"I'll bet I'll wake up, someday, and find out it's all

a dream. You know this kind of thing doesn't really happen — not to a dub like me."

One year; two; three; four. Routine. A little boredom. Some impatience. She began to find fault with the very things she had liked in him: his superneatness; his fondness for dashing suit patterns; his throaty tenor; his worship of her. And the flap. Oh, above all, that flap! That little, innocent, meaningless mannerism that made her tremble with nervousness. She hated it so that she could not trust herself to speak of it to him. That was the trouble. Had she spoken of it, laughingly or in earnest, before it became an obsession with her, that hideous breakfast quarrel, with its taunts, and revilings, and open hate, might never have come to pass.

Terry Platt herself didn't know what was the matter with her. She would have denied that anything was wrong. She didn't even throw her hands above her head and shriek: "I want to live! I want to live! I want to live!" like a lady in a play. She only knew she was sick of sewing at the Wetona West End Red Cross shop; sick of marketing, of home comforts, of Orville, of the flap.

Orville, you may remember, left at 8:19. The 11:23 bore Terry Chicago-ward. She had left the house as it was — beds unmade, rooms unswept, breakfast table uncleared. She intended never to come back.

Now and then a picture of the chaos she had left behind would flash across her order-loving mind. The spoon on the tablecloth.

Orville's pajamas dangling over the bathroom chair. The coffeepot on the gas stove.

"Pooh! What do I care?"

In her pocketbook she had a tidy sum saved out of the housekeeping money. She was naturally thrifty, and Orville had never been niggardly. Her meals when Orville was on the road had been those sketchy, haphazard affairs with which women content themselves when their household is manless. At noon she went into the dining car and ordered a flaunting little repast of chicken salad and asparagus and Neapolitan ice cream. The men in the dining car eyed her speculatively and with appreciation. Then their glance dropped to the third finger of her left hand, and wandered away. She had meant to remove it. In fact, she had taken it off and dropped it into her bag. But her hand felt so queer, so unaccustomed, so naked, that she had found herself slipping the narrow band on again, and her thumb groped for it, gratefully.

It was almost five o'clock when she reached Chicago. She felt no uncertainty or bewilderment. She had been in Chicago three or four times since her marriage. She went to a downtown hotel. It was too late, she told herself, to look for a less expensive room that night. When she had tidied herself she went out. The things she did were the childish, aimless things that one does who finds herself in possession of sudden liberty. She walked up State Street, and stared in the windows; came back, turned into Madison, passed a bright little shop in the window of which taffy-white and gold — was being wound endlessly and fascinatingly about a dou-ble-jointed machine. She went in and bought a sackful, and wandered on down the street, munching.

She had supper at one of those white-tiled sarcophagi that emblazon Chicago's downtown side streets. It had been her original intention to dine in state in the rose-and-gold dining room of her hotel. She had even thought daringly of lobster. But at the last moment she recoiled from the idea of dining alone in that wilderness of tables so obviously meant for two.

After her supper she went to a picture show. She was amazed to find there, instead of the accustomed or-chestra, a pipe organ that panted and throbbed and rumbled over lugubrious classics. The picture was about a faithless wife. Terry left in the middle of it.

She awoke next morning at seven, as usual, started up wildly, looked around, and dropped back. Nothing to get up for. The knowledge did not fill her with a rush of relief. She would have her breakfast in bed. She telephoned for it, languidly. But when it came she got up and ate it from the table, after all.

That morning she found a fairly comfortable room, more within her means, on the North Side in the boardinghouse district. She unpacked and hung up her clothes and drifted downtown again, idly. It was noon when she came to the corner of State and Madison Streets. It was a maelstrom that caught her up, and buffeted her about, and tossed her helplessly this way and that.

*T*he thousands jostled Terry, and knocked her hat awry, and dug her with unheeding elbows, and stepped on her feet.

"Say, look here!" she said once futilely. They did not stop to listen. State and Madison has no time for Terrys from Wetona. It goes its way, pell-mell. If it saw Terry at all it saw her only as a prettyish person, in the wrong kind of suit and hat, with a bewildered, resentful look on her face.

Terry drifted on down the west side of State Street, with the hurrying crowd. State and Monroe. A sound came to Terry's ears.

A sound familiar, beloved. To her ear, harassed with the roar and crash, with the shrill scream of the whistle of the policeman at the crossing, with the hiss of feet shuffling on cement, it was a celestial strain. She looked up, toward the sound. A great second-story window opened wide to the street. In it a girl at a piano, and a man, red-faced, singing through a megaphone. And on a flaring red and green sign:

BERNIE GOTTSCHALK'S MUSIC HOUSE!

COME IN! HEAR BERNIE GOTTSCHALK'S LATEST HIT!
THE HEART-THROB SONG THAT HAS GOT 'EM ALL!
THE SONG THAT MADE THE SQUAREHEADS CRAWL!

*"I come from Paris, Illinois, but oh! you Paris, France!
I used to wear blue overalls but now it's khaki pants."*

COME IN! COME IN!

Terry accepted.

She followed the sound of the music. Around the corner. Up a little flight of stairs. She entered the realm of Euterpe; Euterpe with her hair frizzed; Euterpe with her flowing white robe replaced by soiled white shoes; Euterpe abandoning her flute for jazz. She sat at the piano, a red-haired young lady whose familiarity with the piano had bred contempt. Nothing else could have accounted for her treatment of it. Her fingers, tipped with sharp-pointed and glistening nails, clawed the keys with a dreadful mechanical motion. There were stacks of music sheets on counters and shelves and dangling from overhead wires. The girl at the piano never ceased playing. She played mostly by request.

A prospective purchaser would mumble something in the ear of one of the clerks. The fat man with the megaphone would bawl out, "Hicky Boola, Miss Ryan!" And Miss Ryan would oblige. She made a hideous rattle and crash and clatter of sound.

Terry joined the crowds about the counter. The girl at the piano was not looking at the keys. Her head was screwed around over her left shoulder and as she played she was holding forth animatedly to a girl friend who had evidently dropped in from some store or office during the lunch hour. Now and again the fat man paused in his vocal efforts to reprimand her for her slackness. She paid no heed. There was something gruesome, uncanny, about the way her fingers went their own way over the defenseless keys. Her conversation with the frowzy little girl went on.

"Wha'd he say?" (Over her shoulder.)

"Oh, he laffed."

"Well, didja go?"

"Me! Well, whutya think I yam, anyway?"

"I woulda took a chanst."

The fat man rebelled.

"Look here! Get busy! What are you paid for? Talkin' or playin'? Huh?"

The person at the piano, openly reproved thus before her friend, lifted her uninspired hands from the keys and spake. When she had finished she rose.

"But you can't leave now," the megaphone man argued. "Right in the rush hour."

"I'm gone," said the girl. The fat man looked about, helplessly. He gazed at the abandoned piano, as though it must go on of its own accord. Then at the crowd.

"Where's Miss Schwimmer?" he demanded of a clerk.

"Out to lunch."

Terry pushed her way to the edge of the counter and leaned over. "I can play for you," she said.

The man looked at her. "Sight?"

"Yes."

"Come on."

Terry went around to the other side of the counter, took off her hat and coat, rubbed her hands together briskly, sat down, and began to play. The crowd edged closer.

It is a curious study, this noonday crowd that gathers to sate its music hunger on the scraps vouchsafed it by Bernie Gottschalk's Music House. Loose-lipped, slope-shouldered young men with bad complexions and slender hands. Girls whose clothes are an unconscious satire on present-day fashions. On their faces, as they listen to the music, is a look of peace and dreaming. They stand about, smiling a wistful half smile. The music seems to satisfy a something within them. Faces dull, eyes lusterless, they listen in a sort of trance.

Terry played on. She played as Terry Sheehan used to play. She played as no music hack at Bernie Gottschalk's had ever played before. The crowd swayed a little to the sound of it. Some kept time with little jerks of the shoulder — the little hitching movement of the dancer whose blood is filled with the fever of syncopation. Even the crowd flowing down State Street must have caught the rhythm of it, for the room soon filled.

At two o'clock the crowd began to thin. Business would be slack, now, until five, when it would again pick up until closing time at six. The fat vocalist put down his megaphone, wiped his forehead, and regarded Terry with a warm blue eye. He had just finished singing "I've Wandered Far from Dear Old Mother's Knee." (Bernie Gottschalk Inc. Chicago. New York. You can't get bit with a Gottschalk hit. 15 cents each.)

"Girlie," he said, emphatically, "you sure — can — play!" He came over to her at the piano and put a stubby hand on her shoulder. "Yessir! Those little fingers —"

Terry just turned her head to look down her nose at the moist hand resting on her shoulder. "Those little fingers are going to meet your face if you don't move on."

"Who gave you your job?" demanded the fat man.

"Nobody. I picked it myself. You can have it if you want it."

"Can't you take a joke?"

"Label yours."

As the crowd dwindled she played less feverishly, but there was nothing slipshod about her performance. The chubby songster found time to proffer brief explanations in asides. "They want the patriotic stuff. It used to be all that Hawaiian dope, and Wild Irish Rose stuff, and songs about wanting to go back to every place from Dixie to Duluth. But now seems it's all these here flag wavers. Honestly, I'm so sick of 'em I got a notion to enlist to get away from it."

Terry eyed him with withering briefness. "A little training wouldn't ruin your figure."

She had never objected to Orville's embonpoint. But then, Orville was a different sort of fat man; pink-cheeked, springy, immaculate.

At four o'clock, as she was in the chorus of "Isn't There Another Joan of Arc?" a melting masculine voice from the other side of the counter said "Pardon me. What's that you're playing?"

Terry told him. She did not look up. "I wouldn't have known it. Played like that — a second 'Marseillaise.' If the words — What are the words? Let me see a —"

"Show the gentleman a 'Joan,'" Terry commanded briefly, over her shoulder. The fat man laughed a wheezy laugh. Terry glanced around, still playing, and encountered the gaze of two melting masculine eyes that matched the melting masculine voice. The songster waved a hand uniting Terry and the eyes in informal introduction.

"Mr. Leon Sammett, the gentleman who sings the Gottschalk songs wherever songs are heard. And Mrs.

— that is — and Mrs. Sammett —"

Terry turned. A sleek, swarthy world-old young man with the fashionable concave torso, and alarmingly convex bone-rimmed glasses. Through them his darkly luminous gaze glowed upon Terry. To escape their warmth she sent her own gaze past him to encounter the arctic stare of the large blonde who had been included so lamely in the introduction. And at that the frigidity of that stare softened, melted, dissolved.

"Why, Terry Sheehan! What in the world!"

Terry's eyes bored beneath the layers of flabby fat. "It's — why, it's Ruby Watson, isn't it? Eccentric Song and Dance —"

She glanced at the concave young man and faltered. He was not Jim, of the Bijou days. From him her eyes leaped back to the fur-bedecked splendor of the woman. The plump face went so painfully red that the make-up stood out on it, a distinct layer, like thin ice covering flowing water. As she surveyed that bulk Terry realized that while Ruby might still claim eccentricity, her song-and-dance days were over. "That's ancient history, m' dear. I haven't been working for three years. What're you doing in this joint? I'd heard you'd done well for yourself. That you were married."

"I am. That is I — well, I am. I —"

At that the dark young man leaned over and patted Terry's hand that lay on the counter. He smiled. His own hand was incredibly slender, long, and tapering.

"That's all right," he assured her, and smiled. "You two girls can have a reunion later. What I want to know is can you play by ear?"

"Yes, but —"

He leaned far over the counter. "I knew it the minute I heard you play. You've got the touch. Now listen. See if you can get this, and fake the bass."

He fixed his somber and hypnotic eyes on Terry. His

mouth screwed up into a whistle. The tune — a tawdry but haunting little melody — came through his lips. Terry turned back to the piano. "Of course you know you flatted every note," she said.

This time it was the blonde who laughed, and the man who flushed. Terry cocked her head just a little to one side, like a knowing bird, looked up into space beyond the piano top, and played the lilting little melody with charm and fidelity. The dark young man followed her with a wagging of the head and little jerks of both outspread hands. His expression was beatific, enraptured. He hummed a little under his breath and anyone who was music-wise would have known that he was just a half beat behind her all the way.

When she had finished he sighed deeply, ecstatically. He bent his lean frame over the counter and, despite his swart coloring, seemed to glitter upon her — his eyes, his teeth, his very fingernails.

"Something led me here. I never come up on Tuesdays. But something —"

"You was going to complain," put in his lady, heavily, "about that Teddy Sykes at the Palace Gardens singing the same songs this week that you been boosting at the Inn."

He put up a vibrant, peremptory hand. "Bah! What does that matter now! What does anything matter now! Listen Miss — ah — Miss — ?"

"Pl-Sheehan. Terry Sheehan."

He gazed off a moment into space. "Hm. 'Leon Sammett in Songs.

Miss Terry Sheehan at the Piano.' That doesn't sound bad. Now listen, Miss Sheehan. I'm singing down at the University Inn. The Gottschalk song hits. I guess you know my work. But I want to talk to you, private. It's something to your interest. I go on down at the Inn at six. Will you come and have a little something with Ruby and me? Now?"

"Now?" faltered Terry, somewhat helplessly. Things seemed to be moving rather swiftly for her, accustomed as she was to the peaceful routine of the past four years.

"Get your hat. It's your life chance. Wait till you see your name in two-foot electrics over the front of every big-time house in the country. You've got music in you. Tie to me and you're made." He turned to the woman beside him. "Isn't that so, Rube?"

"Sure. Look at *me!*" One would not have thought there could be so much subtle vindictiveness in a fat blonde.

Sammett whipped out a watch. "Just three quarters of an hour. Come on, girlie."

His conversation had been conducted in an urgent undertone, with side glances at the fat man with the megaphone. Terry approached him now.

"I'm leaving now," she said.

"Oh, no, you're not. Six o'clock is your quitting time."

In which he touched the Irish in Terry. "Anytime I quit is my quitting time. She went in quest of hat and coat much as the girl had done whose place she had taken early in the day. The fat man followed her, protesting. Terry, putting on her hat, tried to ignore him. But he laid one plump hand on her arm and kept it there, though she tried to shake him off.

"Now, listen to me. That boy wouldn't mind grinding his heel on your face if he thought it would bring him up a step. I know'm. See that walking stick he's carrying? Well, compared to the yellow stripe that's in him, that cane is a Lead pencil. He's a song tout, that's all he is." Then, more feverishly, as Terry tried to pull away: "Wait a minute. You're a decent girl. I want to — Why, he can't even sing a note without you give it to him first. He can put a song over, yes. But how? By flashing that toothy grin of his and talking every word of it. Don't you —"

But Terry freed herself with a final jerk and whipped around the counter. The two, who had been talking together in an undertone, turned to welcome her. "We've got a half-hour. Come on. It's just over to Clark and up a block or so."

The University Inn, that gloriously intercollegiate institution which welcomes any graduate of any school of experience, was situated in the basement, down a flight of stairs. Into the unwonted quiet that reigns during the hour of low potentiality, between five and six, the three went, and seated themselves at a table in an obscure corner. A waiter brought them things in little glasses, though no order had been given. The woman who had been Ruby Watson was so silent as to be almost wordless. But the man talked rapidly. He talked well, too. The same quality that enabled him, voiceless though he was, to boost a song to success was making his plea sound plausible in Terry's ears now.

"*I*'ve got to go and make up in a few minutes. So get this. I'm not going to stick down in this basement eating house forever. I've got too much talent. If I only had a voice — I mean a singing voice. But I haven't. But then, neither had Georgie Cohan, and I can't see that it wrecked his life any. Now listen. I've got a song. It's my own. That bit you played for me up at Gottschalk's is part of the chorus. But it's the words that'll go big. They're great. It's an aviation song, see? Airplane stuff. They're yelling that it's the airyoplanes that're going to win this war. Well, I'll help 'em. This song is going to put the aviator where he belongs. It's going to be the big song of the war. It's going to make

'Tipperary' sound like a Moody and Sankey hymn. It's
the —"

Ruby lifted her heavy-lidded eyes and sent him a
meaning look. "Get down to business, Leon. I'll tell
her how good you are while you're making up."

He shot her a malignant glance, but took her advice.
"Now what I've been looking for for years is somebody
who has got the music knack to give me the accompaniment just a quarter of a jump ahead of my voice, see?
I can follow like a lamb, but I've got to have that feeler
first. It's more than a knack. It's a gift. And you've got
it. I know it when I see it. I want to get away from this
night-club thing. There's nothing in it for a man of
my talent. I'm gunning for bigger game. But they won't
sign me without a tryout. And when they hear my voice
they — Well, if me and you work together we can fool
'em. The song's great. And my make-up's one of these
aviation costumes to go with the song, see? Pants tight
in the knee and baggy on the hips. And a coat with
one of those full-skirt whaddyoucall'ems —"

"Peplums," put in Ruby, placidly.

"Sure. And the girls'll be wild about it. And the
words!" He began to sing, gratingly off key:

Put on your sky clothes,
Put on your fly clothes,
And take a trip with me.
We'll sail so high
Up in the sky
We'll drop a bomb from Mercury.

"Why, that's awfully cute!" exclaimed Terry. Until
now her opinion of Mr. Sammett's talents had not
been on a level with his.

"Yeah, but wait till you hear the second verse. That's
only part of the chorus. You see, he's supposed to be
talking to a French girl. He says:

'I'll parlez-vous in Francais plain
  You'll answer, "Cher Americain,"
  We'll both . . .'"

The six-o'clock lights blazed up suddenly. A sad-looking group of men trailed in and made for a corner where certain bulky, shapeless bundles were soon revealed as those glittering and tortuous instruments which go to make a jazz band.

"You better go, Lee. The crowd comes in awful early now, with all these buyers in town."

Both hands on the table, he half rose, reluctantly, still talking. "I've got three other songs. They make Gottschalk's stuff look sick. All I want's a chance. What I want you to do is accompaniment. On the stage, see? Grand piano. And a swell set. I haven't quite made up my mind to it. But a kind of an army camp room, see? And maybe you dressed as Liberty. Anyway, it'll be new, and a knockout. If only we can get away with the voice thing. Say, if Eddie Foy, all those years never had a —"

The band opened with a terrifying clash of cymbal and thump of drum. "Back at the end of my first turn," he said as he Red. Terry followed his lithe, electric figure. She turned to meet the heavy-lidded gaze of the woman seated opposite. She relaxed, then, and sat back with a little sigh. "Well! If he talks that way to the managers I don't see —"

Ruby laughed a mirthless little laugh. "Talk doesn't get it over with the managers, honey. You've got to deliver."

"Well, but he's — that song is a good one. I don't say it's as good as he thinks it is, but it's good."

"Yes," admitted the woman, grudgingly, "it's good."

"Well, then?"

The woman beckoned a waiter; he nodded and vanished, and reappeared with a glass that was twin to the one she had just emptied. "Does he look like he knew French? Or could make a rhyme?"

"But didn't he? Doesn't he?"

"The words were written by a little French girl who used to skate down here last winter, when the craze was on. She was stuck on a Chicago kid who went over to fly for the French."

"But the music?"

"There was a Russian girl who used to dance in the cabaret and she —"

Terry's head came up with a characteristic little jerk. "I don't believe it!"

"Better." She gazed at Terry with the drowsy look that was so different from the quick, clear glance of the Ruby Watson who used to dance so nimbly in the old Bijou days. "What'd you and your husband quarrel about, Terry?"

Terry was furious to feel herself flushing. "Oh, nothing. He just — I — it was — Say, how did you know we'd quarreled?"

And suddenly all the fat woman's apathy dropped from her like a garment and some of the old sparkle and animation illumined her heavy face. She pushed her glass aside and leaned forward on her folded arms, so that her face was close to Terry's.

"Terry Sheehan, I know you've quarreled, and I know just what it was about. Oh, I don't mean the very thing it was about; but the kind of thing. I'm going to do something for you, Terry, that I wouldn't take the trouble to do for most women. But I guess I ain't had all the softness knocked out of me yet, though it's a wonder. And I guess I remember too plain the decent kid you was in the old days. What was the name of that little small-time house me and Jim used to play? Bijou, that's it; Bijou."

The band struck up a new tune. Leon Sammett — slim, sleek, lithe in his evening clothes — appeared with a little fair girl in pink chiffon. The woman reached across the table and put one pudgy, jeweled hand on Terry's arm. "He'll be through in ten minutes. Now listen to me. I left Jim four years ago, and there hasn't been a minute since then, day or night, when I wouldn't have crawled back to him on my hands and knees if I could. But I couldn't. He wouldn't have me now. How could he? How do I know you've quarreled? I can see it in your eyes. They look just the way mine have felt for four years, that's how. I met up with this boy, and there wasn't anybody to do the turn for me that I'm trying to do for you. Now get this. I left Jim because when he ate corn on the cob he always closed his eyes and it drove me wild. Don't laugh."

"I'm not laughing," said Terry.

"Women are like that. One night — we was playing Fond du Lac; I remember just as plain — we was eating supper before the show and Jim reached for one of those big yellow ears, and buttered and salted it, and me kind of hanging on to the edge of the table with my nails. Seemed to me if he shut his eyes when he put his teeth into that ear of corn I'd scream. And he did. And I screamed. And that's all."

Terry sat staring at her with a wide-eyed stare, like a sleepwalker. Then she wet her lips slowly. "But that's almost the very —"

"Kid, go on back home. I don't know whether it's too late or not, but go anyway. If you've lost him I suppose it ain't anymore than you deserve; but I hope to God you don't get your deserts this time. He's almost through. If he sees you going he can't quit in the middle of his song to stop you. He'll know I put you wise, and he'll prob'ly half kill me for it. But it's worth it. You get."

And Terry — dazed, shaking, but grateful — fled. Down the noisy aisle, up the stairs, to the street. Back to her rooming house. Out again, with her suitcase, and into the right railroad station somehow, at last. Not another Wetona train until midnight. She shrank into a remote corner of the waiting room and there she huddled until midnight, watching the entrances like a child who is fearful of ghosts in the night.

The hands of the station clock seemed fixed and immovable. The hour between eleven and twelve was endless. She was on the train. It was almost morning. It was morning. Dawn was breaking. She was home! She had the house key clutched tightly in her hand long before she turned Schroeder's corner. Suppose he had come home! Suppose he had jumped a town and come home ahead of his schedule. They had quarreled once before, and he had done that.

Up the front steps. Into the house. Not a sound. She stood there a moment in the early-morning half-light. She peered into the dining room. The table, with its breakfast debris, was as she had left it. In the kitchen the coffeepot stood on the gas stove. She was home. She was safe. She ran up the stairs, got out of her clothes and into gingham morning things. She flung open windows everywhere. Downstairs once more she plunged into an orgy of cleaning. Dishes, table, stove, floor, rugs. She washed, scoured, swabbed, polished. By eight o'clock she had done the work that would ordinarily have taken until noon. The house was shining, orderly, and redolent of soapsuds.

During all this time she had been listening, listening, with her subconscious ear. Listening for something she had refused to name definitely in her mind, but listening, just the same; waiting.

And then, at eight o'clock, it came. The rattle of a key in the lock. The boom of the front door. Firm footsteps.

He did not go to meet her, and she did not go to meet him. They came together and were in each other's arms. She was weeping.

"Now, now, old girl. What's there to cry about? Don't, honey; don't. It's all right." She raised her head then, to look at him. How fresh and rosy and big he seemed, after that little sallow restaurant rat.

"How did you get here? How did you happen — ?"

"Jumped all the way from Ashland. Couldn't get a sleeper, so I sat up all night. I had to come back and square things with you, Terry. My mind just wasn't on my work. I kept thinking how I'd talked — how I'd talked —"

"Oh, Orville, don't! I can't bear — Have you had your breakfast?"

"Why, no. The train was an hour late. You know that Ashland train."

But she was out of his arms and making for the kitchen. "You go and clean up. I'll have hot biscuits and everything in no time. You poor boy. No breakfast!"

She made good her promise. It could not have been more than half an hour later when he was buttering his third feathery, golden-brown biscuit. But she had eaten nothing. She watched him, and listened, and again her eyes were somber, but for a different reason. He broke open his egg. His elbow came up just a fraction of an inch. Then he remembered, and flushed like a schoolboy, and brought it down again, carefully. And at that she gave a tremulous cry, and rushed around the table to him.

"Oh, Orville!" She took the offending elbow in her two arms, and bent and kissed the rough coat sleeve.

"Why, Terry! Don't, honey. Don't!"

"Oh, Orville, listen —"

"Yes."

"Listen, Orville —"

"I'm listening, Terry."

"I've got something to tell you. There's something you've got to know."

"Yes, I know it, Terry. I knew you'd out with it, pretty soon, if I just waited."

She lifted an amazed face from his shoulder then, and stared at him. "But how could you know? You couldn't! How could you?"

He patted her shoulder then, gently. "I can always tell. When you have something on your mind you always take up a spoon of coffee, and look at it, and kind of joggle it back and forth in the spoon, and then dribble it back into the cup again, without once tasting it. It used to get me nervous, when we were first married, watching you. But now I know it just means you're worried about something, and I wait, and pretty soon —"

"Oh, Orville!" she cried then. "Oh, Orville!"

"Now, Terry. Just spill it, hon. Just spill it to Daddy. And you'll feel better."

Farmer in the Dell

Old Ben Westerveld was taking it easy. Every muscle taut, every nerve tense, his keen eyes vainly straining to pierce the blackness of the stuffy room — there lay Ben Westerveld in bed, taking it easy. And it was hard. Hard. He wanted to get up. He wanted so intensely to get up that the mere effort of lying there made him ache all over. His toes were curled with the effort. His fingers were clenched with it. His breath came short, and his thighs felt cramped. Nerves. But old Ben Westerveld didn't know that. What should a retired and well-to-do farmer of fifty-eight know of nerves, especially when he has moved to the city and is taking it easy?

If only he knew what time it was. Here in Chicago you couldn't tell whether it was four o'clock or seven unless you looked at your watch. To do that it was necessary to turn on the light. And to turn on the light meant that he would turn on, too, a flood of querulous protest from his wife, Bella, who lay asleep beside him.

When for forty-five years of your life you have risen at four-thirty daily, it is difficult to learn to loll. To do it successfully, you must be a natural-born loller to begin with and revert. Bella Westerveld was and had. So there she lay, asleep. Old Ben wasn't and hadn't. So there he lay, terribly wide-awake, wondering what made his heart thump so fast when he was lying so still. If it had been light, you could have seen the lines of strained resignation in the sagging muscles of his patient face.

They had lived in the city for almost a year, but it was the same every morning. He would open his eyes, start up with one hand already reaching for the limp, drab work-worn garments that used to drape the chair by his bed. Then he would remember and sink back while a great wave of depression swept over him. Nothing to get up for. Store clothes on the chair by the bed. He was taking it easy.

Back home on the farm in southern Illinois he had known the hour the instant his eyes opened. Here the flat next door was so close that the bedroom was in twilight even at midday. On the farm he could tell by the feeling — an intangible thing, but infallible. He could gauge the very quality of the blackness that comes just before dawn. The crowing of the cocks, the stamping of the cattle, the twittering of the birds in the old elm whose branches were etched eerily against his window in the ghostly light — these things he had never needed. He had known. But here in the un-sylvan section of Chicago which bears the bosky name of Englewood, the very darkness had a strange quality.

A hundred unfamiliar noises misled him. There were no cocks, no cattle, no elm. Above all, there was no instinctive feeling. Once, when they first came to the city, he had risen at twelve-thirty, thinking it was morning, and had gone clumping about the flat, waking up everyone and loosing from his wife's lips a stream of acid vituperation that seared even his case-hardened sensibilities. The people sleeping in the bedroom of the flat next door must have heard her.

"You big rube! Getting up in the middle of the night and stomping around like cattle. You'd better build a shed in the back yard and sleep there if you're so dumb you can't tell night from day."

Even after thirty-three years of marriage he had never ceased to be appalled at the coarseness of her mind and speech — she who had seemed so mild and fragile and exquisite when he married her. He had crept back to bed shamefacedly. He could hear the couple in the bedroom of the flat just across the little court grumbling and then laughing a little, grudgingly, and yet with appreciation. That bedroom, too, had still the power to appall him. Its nearness, its forced intimacy, were daily shocks to him whose most immediate neighbor, back on the farm, had been a quarter of a mile away. The sound of a shoe dropped on the hardwood floor, the rush of water in the bathroom, the murmur of nocturnal confidences, the fretful cry of a child in the night, all startled and distressed him whose ear had found music in the roar of the thresher and had been soothed by the rattle of the tractor and the hoarse hoot of the steamboat whistle at the landing. His farm's edge had been marked by the Mississippi rolling grandly by.

Since they had moved into town, he had found only one city sound that he really welcomed — the rattle and clink that marked the milkman's matutinal visit. The milkman came at six, and he was the good fairy who released Ben Westerveld from durance vile — or had until the winter months made his coming later and later, so that he became worse than useless as a timepiece. But now it was late March, and mild. The milkman's coming would soon again mark old Ben's rising hour. Before he had begun to take it easy, six o'clock had seen the entire mechanism of his busy little world humming smoothly and sweetly, the whole set in motion by his own big work-callused hands. Those hands puzzled him now. He often looked at them curiously and in a detached sort of way, as if they belonged to someone else. So white they were, and smooth and soft, with long, pliant nails that never broke off from rough work as they used to. Of late there were little splotches of brown on the backs of his hands and around the thumbs.

"Guess it's my liver," he decided, rubbing the spots thoughtfully. "She gets kind of sluggish from me not doing anything. Maybe a little spring tonic wouldn't go bad. Tone me up."

He got a little bottle of reddish-brown mixture from the druggist on Halstead Street near Sixty-third. A genial gendeman, the druggist, white-coated and dapper, stepping affably about the fragrant-smelling store. The reddish-brown mixture had toned old Ben up surprisingly — while it lasted. He had two bottles of it. But on discontinuing it he slumped back into his old apathy.

Ben Westerveld, in his store clothes, his clean blue shirt, his incongruous hat, ambling aimlessly about Chicago's teeming, gritty streets, was a tragedy. Those big, capable hands, now dangling so limply from inert wrists, had wrested a living from the soil; those strangely unfaded blue eyes had the keenness of vision which comes from scanning great stretches of earth and sky; the stocky, square-shouldered body suggested power unutilized. All these spelled tragedy. Worse than tragedy — waste.

For almost half a century this man had combated the elements, head set, eyes wary, shoulders squared. He had fought wind and sun, rain and drought, scourge and flood. He had risen before dawn and slept before sunset. In the process he had taken on something of the color and the rugged immutability of the fields and hills and trees among which he toiled. Something of their dignity, too, though your town dweller might fail to see it beneath the drab exterior. He had about him none of the highlights and sharp points of the city man. He seemed to blend in with the background of nature so as to be almost undistinguishable from it, as were the furred and feathered creatures. This farmer differed from the city man as a hillock differs from an artificial golf bunker, though form and substance are the same.

Ben Westerveld didn't know he was a tragedy. Your farmer is not given to introspection. For that matter, anyone knows that a farmer in town is a comedy. Vaudeville, burlesque, the Sunday supplement, the comic papers, have marked him a fair target for ridicule. Perhaps one should know him in his overalled, stubble-bearded days, with the rich black loam of the Mississippi bottomlands clinging to his boots.

At twenty-five, given a tasseled cap, doublet and hose, and a long, slim pipe, Ben Westerveld would have been the prototype of one of those rollicking, lusty young mynheers that laugh out at you from a Frans Hals canvas. A roguish fellow with a merry eye; red-cheeked, vigorous. A serious mouth, though, and great sweetness of expression. As he grew older, the seriousness crept up and up and almost entirely obliterated the roguishness. By the time the life of ease claimed him, even the ghost of that ruddy wight of boyhood had vanished.

The Westerveld ancestry was as Dutch as the name. It had been hundreds of years since the first Westervelds came to America, and they had married and intermarried until the original Holland strain had almost entirely disappeared. They had drifted to southern Illinois by one of those slow processes of migration and had settled in Calhoun County, then almost a wilderness, but magnificent with its rolling hills, majestic rivers, and gold-and-purple distances. But to the practical Westerveld mind, hills and rivers and purple haze existed only in their relation to crops and weather. Ben, though, had a way of turning his face up to the sky sometimes, and it was not to scan the heavens for clouds. You saw him leaning on the plow handle to watch the whirring flight of a partridge across the meadow. He liked farming. Even the drudgery of it never made him grumble. He was a natural farmer as men are natural mechanics or musicians or salesmen. Things grew for him. He seemed instinctively to know facts about the kin ship of soil and seed that other men had to learn from books or experience. It grew to be a saying in that section that "Ben Westerveld could grow a crop on rock."

At picnics and neighborhood frolics Ben could throw farther and run faster and pull harder than any of the other farmer boys who took part in the rough games. And he could pick up a girl with one hand and hold her at arm's length while she shrieked with pretended fear and real ecstasy. The girls all liked Ben. There was that almost primitive strength which appealed to the untamed in them as his gentleness appealed to their softer side. He liked the girls, too, and could have had his pick of them. He teased them all, took them buggy riding, beaued them about to neighbor-hood parties. But by the time he was twenty-five the thing had narrowed down to the Byers girl on the farm adjoining Westerveld's. There was what the neighbors called an understanding, though perhaps he had never actually asked the Byers girl to marry him. You saw him going down the road toward the Byers place four nights out of the seven. He had a quick, light step at variance with his sturdy build, and very different from the heavy, slouching gait of the work-weary farmer. He had a habit of carrying in his hand a little twig or switch cut from a tree. This he would twirl blithely as he walked along. The switch and the twirl represented just so much energy and animal spirits. He never so much as flicked a dandelion head with it.

An inarticulate sort of thing, that courtship.

"Hello, Emma."

"How do, Ben."

"Thought you might like to walk a piece down the road. They got a calf at Aug Tietjens' with five legs."

"I heard. I'd just as lief walk a little piece. I'm kind of beat, though. We've got the threshers day after tomorrow. We've been cooking up."

Beneath Ben's bonhomie and roguishness there was much shyness. The two would plod along the road together in a sort of blissful agony of embarrassment. The neighbors were right in their surmise that there was no definite understanding between them. But the thing was settled in the minds of both. Once Ben had said: "Pop says I can have the north eighty on easy payments if – when –"

Emma Byers had flushed up brightly, but had answered equally: "That's a fine piece. Your pop is an awful good man."

The stolid exteriors of these two hid much that was fine and forceful. Emma Byers' thoughtful forehead and intelligent eyes would have revealed that in her. Her mother was dead. She kept house for her father and brother. She was known as "that smart Byers girl." Her butter and eggs and garden stuff brought higher prices at Commercial, twelve miles away, than did any other's in the district. She was not a pretty girl, according to the local standards, but there was about her, even at twenty-two, a clear-headedness and a restful serenity that promised well for Ben Westerveld's future happiness.

But Ben Westerveld's future was not to lie in Emma Byers' capable hands. He knew that as soon as he saw Bella Huckins. Bella Huckins was the daughter of old "Red Front" Huckins, who ran the saloon of that cheerful name in Commercial. Bella had elected to teach school, not from any bent toward learning but because teaching appealed to her as being a rather elegant occupation. The Huckins family was not elegant. In that day a year or two of teaching in a country school took the place of the present-day normal-school diploma. Bella had an eye on St. Louis, forty miles from the town of Commercial. So she used the country school as a step toward her ultimate goal, though she hated the country and dreaded her apprenticeship.

"I'll get a beau," she said, "who'll take me driving and around. And Saturdays and Sundays I can come to town."

The first time Ben Westerveld saw her she was coming down the road toward him in her tight-fitting black alpaca dress. The sunset was behind her. Her hair was very golden. In a day of tiny waists hers could have been spanned by Ben Westerveld's two hands. He discovered that later. Just now he thought he had never seen anything so fairylike and dainty, though he did not put it that way. Ben was not glib of thought or speech.

He knew at once this was the new schoolteacher. He had heard of her coming, though at the time the conversation had interested him not at all. Bella knew who he was, too. She had learned the name and history of every eligible young man in the district two days after her arrival. That was due partly to her own bold curiosity and partly to the fact that she was boarding with the Widow Becker, the most notorious gossip in the county. In Bella's mental list of the neighborhood swains Ben Westerveld already occupied a position at the top of the column.

He felt his face redden as they approached each other. To hide his embarrassment he swung his little hickory switch gaily and called to his dog Dunder, who was nosing about by the roadside. Dunder bounded forward, spied the newcomer, and leaped toward her playfully and with natural canine curiosity.

Bella screamed. She screamed and ran to Ben and clung to him, clasping her hands about his arm. Ben lifted the hickory switch in his free hand and struck Dunder a sharp cut with it. It was the first time in his life that he had done such a thing. If he had had a sane moment from that time until the day he married Bella Huckins, he never would have forgotten the dumb hurt in Dunder's stricken eyes and shrinking, quivering body.

Bella screamed again, still clinging to him. Ben was saying: "He won't hurt you. He won't hurt you," meanwhile patting her shoulder reassuringly. He looked down at her pale face. She was so slight, so childlike, so apparently different from the sturdy country girls. From — well, from the girls he knew. Her helplessness, her utter femininity, appealed to all that was masculine in him. Bella, the experienced, clinging to him, felt herself swept from head to foot by a queer electric tingling that was very pleasant but that still had in it something of the sensation of a wholesale bumping of one's crazy bone. If she had been anything but a stupid little flirt, she would have realized that here was a specimen of the virile male with which she could not trifle. She glanced up at him now, smiling faintly. "My, I was scared!" She stepped away from him a little — very little.

"Aw, he wouldn't hurt a flea."

But Bella looked over her shoulder fearfully to where Dunder stood by the roadside, regarding Ben with a look of uncertainty. He still thought that perhaps this was a new game. Not a game that he cared for, but still one to be played if his master fancied it. Ben stooped, picked up a stone, and threw it at Dunder, striking him in the flank.

"Go on home!" he commanded sternly. "Go home!" He started toward the dog with a well-feigned gesture of menace. Dunder, with a low howl, put his tail between his legs and loped off home, a disillusioned dog.

Bella stood looking up at Ben. Ben looked down at her. "You're the new teacher, ain't you?"

"Yes. I guess you must think I'm a fool, going on like a baby about that dog."

"Most girls would be scared of him if they didn't know he wouldn't hurt nobody. He's pretty big."

He paused a moment, awkwardly. "My name's Ben Westerveld."

"Pleased to meet you," said Bella. "Which way was you going? There's a dog down at Tietjens' that's enough to scare anybody. He looks like a pony, he's so big."

"I forgot something at the school this afternoon, and I was walking over to get it." Which was a lie. "I hope it won't get dark before I get there. You were going the other way, weren't you?"

"Oh, I wasn't going no place in particular. I'll be pleased to keep you company down to the school and back." He was surprised at his own sudden masterfulness.

They set off together, chatting as freely as if they had known one another for years. Ben had been on his way to the Byers farm, as usual. The Byers farm and Emma Byers passed out of his mind as completely as if they had been whisked away on a magic rug.

Bella Huckins had never meant to marry him. She

hated farm life.

She was contemptuous of farmer folk. She loathed cooking and drudgery. The Huckinses lived above the saloon in Commercial and Mrs. Huckins was always boiling ham and tongue and cooking pigs' feet and shredding cabbage for slaw, all these edibles being destined for the free-lunch counter downstairs. Bella had early made up her mind that there should be no boiling and stewing and frying in her life. Whenever she could find an excuse she loitered about the saloon. There she found life and talk and color. Old Red Front Huckins used to chase her away, but she always turned up again, somehow, with a dish for the lunch counter or with an armful of clean towels.

Ben Westerveld never said clearly to himself, "I want to marry Bella." He never dared meet the thought. He intended honestly to marry Emma Byers. But this thing was too strong for him. As for Bella, she laughed at him, but she was scared, too. They both fought the thing, she selfishly, he unselfishly, for the Byers girl, with her clear, calm eyes and her dependable ways, was heavy on his heart. Ben's appeal for Bella was merely that of the magnetic male. She never once thought of his finer qualities. Her appeal for him was that of the frail and alluring woman. But in the end they married. The neighborhood was rocked with surprise.

Usually in a courtship it is the male who assumes the bright colors of pretense in order to attract a mate. But Ben Westerveld had been too honest to be anything but himself. He was so honest and fundamentally truthful that he refused at first to allow himself to believe that this slovenly shrew was the fragile and exquisite creature he had married. He had the habit of personal cleanliness, had Ben, in a day when tubbing was a ceremony in an environment that made bodily nicety difficult. He discovered that Bella almost never

washed and that her appearance of fragrant immacu-
lateness, when dressed, was due to a natural clearness
of skin and eye, and to the way her blond hair swept
away in a clean line from her forehead. For the rest,
she was a slattern, with a vocabulary of invective that
would have been a credit to any of the habitués of old
Red Front Huckins' bar.

They had three children, a girl and two boys. Ben
Westerveld prospered in spite of his wife. As the years
went on he added eighty acres here, eighty acres there,
until his land swept down to the very banks of the
Mississippi. There is no doubt that she hindered him
greatly, but he was too expert a farmer to fail. At
threshing time the crew looked forward to working for
Ben, the farmer, and dreaded the meals prepared by
Bella, his wife. She was notoriously the worst cook and
housekeeper in the county. And all through the years,
in trouble and in happiness, her plaint was the same
— "If I'd thought I was going to stick down on a farm
all my life, slavin' for a pack of menfolks day and night,
I'd rather have died. Might as well be dead as rottin'
here."

Her schoolteacher English had early reverted. Her
speech was as slovenly as her dress. She grew stout, too,
and unwieldy, and her skin coarsened from lack of care
and from overeating. And in her children's ears she
continually dinned a hatred of farm life and farming.
"You can get away from it," she counseled her daughter,
Minnie. "Don't you be a rube like your pa," she cau-
tioned John, the older boy. And they profited by her
advice. Minnie went to work in Commercial when she
was seventeen, an overdeveloped girl with an inordi-
nate love of cheap finery. At twenty, she married an
artisan, a surly fellow with roving tendencies. They
moved from town to town. He never stuck long at one
job. John, the older boy, was as much his mother's son

as Minnie was her mother's daughter. Restless, dissatisfied, empty-headed, he was the despair of his father. He drove the farm horses as if they were racers, lashing them up hill and down dale. He was forever lounging off to the village or wheedling his mother for money to take him to Commercial. It was before the day of the ubiquitous automobile. Given one of those present adjuncts to farm life, John would have ended his career much earlier. As it was, they found him lying by the roadside at dawn one morning after the horses had trotted into the yard with the wreck of the buggy bumping the road behind them. He had stolen the horses out of the barn after the help was asleep, had led them stealthily down the road, and then had whirled off to a rendezvous of his own in town. The fall from the buggy might not have hurt him, but evidently he had been dragged almost a mile before his battered body became somehow disentangled from the splintered wood and the reins.

That horror might have served to bring Ben Westerveld and his wife together, but it did not. It only increased her bitterness and her hatred of the locality and the life.

"I hope you're good an' satisfied now," she repeated in endless reproach. "I hope you're good an' satisfied. You was bound you'd make a farmer out of him, an' now you finished the job. You better try your hand at Dike now for a change."

Dike was young Ben, sixteen; and old Ben had no need to try his hand at him. Young Ben was a born farmer, as was his father. He had come honestly by his nickname. In face, figure, expression, and manner he was a five-hundred-year throwback to his Holland ancestors. Apple-cheeked, stocky, merry of eye, and somewhat phlegmatic. When, at school, they had come to the story of the Dutch boy who saved his town from flood by thrusting his finger into the hole in the dike and holding it there until help came, the class, after one look at the accompanying picture in the reader, dubbed young Ben "Dike" Westerveld. And Dike he remained.

Between Dike and his father there was a strong but unspoken feeling. The boy was cropwise, as his father had been at his age. On Sundays you might see the two walking about the farm, looking at the pigs — great black fellows worth almost their weight in silver; eying the stock; speculating on the winter wheat showing dark green in April, with rich patches that were almost black. Young Dike smoked a solemn and judicious pipe, spat expertly, and voiced the opinion that the winter wheat was a fine prospect Ben Westerveld, listening tolerantly to the boy's opinions, felt a great surge of joy that he did not show. Here, at last, was compensation for all the misery and sordidness and bitter disappointment of his married life.

That married life had endured now for more than thirty years. Ben Westerveld still walked with a light, quick step — for his years. The stocky, broad-shouldered figure was a little shrunken. He was as neat and clean at fifty-five as he had been at twenty-five-a habit that, on a farm, is fraught with difficulties. The community knew and respected him. He was a man of standing. When he drove into town on a bright winter morning, in his big sheepskin coat and his shaggy cap and his great boots, and entered the First National Bank, even Shumway, the cashier, would look up from his desk to say:

"Hello, Westerveld! Hello! Well, how goes it?"

When Shumway greeted a farmer in that way you knew that there were no unpaid notes to his discredit.

All about Ben Westerveld stretched the fruit of his toil; the work of his hands. Orchards, fields, cattle, barns, silos. All these things were dependent on him for their future well-being — on him and on Dike after him. His days were full and running over. Much of the work was drudgery; most of it was backbreaking and laborious. But it was his place. It was his reason for being. And he felt that the reason was good, though he never put that thought into words, mental or spoken. He only knew that he was part of the great scheme of things and that he was functioning ably. If he had expressed himself at all, he might have said:

"Well, I got my work cut out for me, and I do it, and do it right."

There was a tractor, now, of course; and a sturdy, middle-class automobile in which Bella lolled red-faced when they drove into town.

As Ben Westerveld had prospered, his shrewish wife had reaped her benefits. Ben was not the selfish type of farmer who insists on twentieth-century farm implements and medieval household equipment. He had added a bedroom here, a cool summer kitchen there, an icehouse, a commodious porch, a washing machine, even a bathroom. But Bella remained unplacated. Her face was set toward the city. And slowly, surely, the effect of thirty years of nagging was beginning to tell on Ben Westerveld. He was the finer metal, but she was the heavier, the coarser. She beat him and molded him as iron beats upon gold.

Minnie was living in Chicago now — a good-natured creature, but slack like her mother. Her surly husband was still talking of his rights and crying down with the rich. They had two children.

Minnie wrote of them, and of the delights of city life. Movies every night. Halsted Street just around the corner. The big stores. State Street. The el took you downtown in no time. Something going on all the while. Bella Westerveld, after one of those letters, was more than a chronic shrew; she became a terrible termagant.

When Ben Westerveld decided to concentrate on hogs and wheat he didn't dream that a world would be clamoring for hogs and wheat for four long years. When the time came, he had them, and sold them fabulously. But wheat and hogs and markets became negligible things on the day that Dike, with seven other farm boys from the district, left for the nearest training camp that was to fit them for France and war.

Bella made the real fuss, wailing and mouthing and going into hysterics. Old Ben took it like a stoic. He drove the boy to town that day. When the train pulled out, you might have seen, if you had looked close, how the veins and cords swelled in the lean brown neck above the clean blue shirt. But that was all. As the weeks went on, the quick, light step began to lag a little. He had lost more than a son; his right-hand helper was gone. There were no farm helpers to be had. Old Ben couldn't do it all. A touch of rheumatism that winter half crippled him for eight weeks. Bella's voice seemed never to stop its plaint.

"There ain't no sense in you trying to make out alone. Next thing you'll die on me, and then I'll have the whole shebang on my hands." At that he eyed her dumbly from his chair by the stove. His resistance was wearing down. He knew it. He wasn't dying. He knew that, too. But something in him was. Something that had resisted her all these years. Something that had made him master and superior in spite of everything.

In those days of illness, as he sat by the stove, the memory of Emma Byers came to him often. She had left that district twenty-eight years ago, and had married, and lived in Chicago somewhere, he had heard, and was prosperous. He wasted no time in idle regrets. He had been a fool, and he paid the price of fools.

Bella, slamming noisily about the room, never suspected the presence in the untidy place of a third person — a sturdy girl of twenty-two or -three, very wholesome to look at, and with honest, intelligent eyes and a serene brow.

"It'll get worse an' worse all the time," Bella's whine went on. "Everybody says the war'll last prob'ly for years an' years. You can't make out alone. Everything's goin' to rack and ruin. You could rent out the farm for a year, on trial. The Burdickers'd take it, and glad. They got those three strappin' louts that's all flat-footed or slab-sided or cross-eyed or somethin', and no good for the army. Let them run it on shares. Maybe they'll even buy, if things turn out. Maybe Dike'll never come b —"

But at the look on his face then, and at the low growl of unaccustomed rage that broke from him, even she ceased her clatter.

They moved to Chicago in the early spring. The look that had been on Ben Westerveld's face when he drove Dike to the train that carried him to camp was stamped there again — indelibly this time, it seemed. Calhoun County in the spring has much the beauty of California. There is a peculiar golden light about it, and the hills are a purplish haze. Ben Westerveld, walking down his path to the gate, was more poignantly dramatic than any figure in a rural play. He did not turn to look back, though, as they do in a play. He dared not.

They rented a flat in Englewood, Chicago, a block from Minnie's. Bella was almost amiable these days. She took to city life as though the past thirty years had never been. White kid shoes, delicatessen stores, the movies, the haggling with peddlers, the crowds, the crashing noise, the cramped, unnatural mode of living — necessitated by a four-room flat — all these urban adjuncts seemed as natural to her as though she had been bred in the midst of them.

She and Minnie used to spend whole days in useless shopping. Theirs was a respectable neighborhood of well-paid artisans, bookkeepers, and small shopkeepers. The women did their own housework in drab garments and soiled boudoir caps that hid a multitude of unkempt heads. They seemed to find a great deal of time for amiable, empty gabbling From seven to four you might see a pair of boudoir caps leaning from opposite bedroom windows, conversing across back porches, pausing in the task of sweeping front steps, standing at a street corner, laden with grocery bundles. Minnie wasted hours in what she called "running over to Ma's for a minute." The two quarreled a great deal, being so nearly of a nature. But the very qualities that combated each other seemed, by some strange chemical process, to bring them together as well.

"I'm going downtown today to do a little shopping," Minnie would say. "Do you want to come along, Ma?"

"What you got to get?"

"Oh, I thought I'd look at a couple little dresses for Pearlie."

"When I was your age I made every stitch you wore."

"Yeh, I bet they looked like it, too. This ain't the farm. I got all I can do to tend to the house, without sewing."

"I did it. I did the housework and the sewin' and cookin', an' besides —"

"A swell lot of housekeepin' you did. You don't need to tell me."

The bickering grew to a quarrel. But in the end they took the downtown el together. You saw them, flushed of face, with twitching fingers, indulging in a sort of orgy of dime spending in the five-and-ten-cent store on the wrong side of State Street.

They pawed over bolts of cheap lace and bits of stuff in the stifling air of the crowded place. They would buy a sack of salted peanuts from the great mound in the glass case, or a bag of the greasy pink candy piled in profusion on the counter, and this they would munch as they went.

They came home late, fagged and irritable, and supplemented their hurried dinner with hastily bought food from the near-by delicatessen.

Thus ran the life of ease for Ben Westerveld, retired farmer. And so now he lay impatiently in bed, rubbing a nervous forefinger over the edge of the sheet and saying to himself that, well, here was another day. What day was it? L'see now. Yesterday was — yesterday. A little feeling of panic came over him. He couldn't remember what yesterday had been. He counted back laboriously and decided that today must be Thursday. Not that it made any difference.

They had lived in the city almost a year now. But the city had not digested Ben. He was a leathery morsel that could not be assimilated. There he stuck in Chicago's crop, contributing nothing, gaining nothing. A rube in a comic collar ambling aimlessly about Halsted Street or State downtown. You saw him conversing hungrily with the gritty and taciturn Swede who was janitor for the block of red-brick flats. Ben used to follow him around pathetically, engaging him in the talk of the day. Ben knew no men except the surly Gus, Minnie's husband. Gus, the firebrand, thought Ben hardly worthy of his contempt. If Ben thought, sometimes, of the respect with which he had always been greeted when he clumped down the main street of Commercial — if he thought of how the farmers for miles around had come to him for expert advice and opinion — he said nothing.

Sometimes the janitor graciously allowed Ben to attend to the furnace of the building in which he lived. He took out ashes, shoveled coal. He tinkered and rattled and shook things. You heard him shoveling and scraping down there, and smelled the acrid odor of his pipe. It gave him something to do. He would emerge sooty and almost happy.

"You been monkeying with that furnace again!" Bella would scold. "If you want something to do, why don't you plant a garden in the back yard and grow something? You was crazy about it on the farm."

His face flushed a slow, dull red at that. He could not explain to her that he lost no dignity in his own eyes in fussing about an inadequate little furnace, but that self-respect would not allow him to stoop to gardening — he who had reigned over six hundred acres of bountiful soil.

On winter afternoons you saw him sometimes at the movies, whiling away one of his many idle hours in the dim, close-smelling atmosphere of the place. Tokyo and Rome and Gallipoli came to him. He saw beautiful tiger-women twining fair, false arms about the stalwart but yielding forms of young men with cleft chins. He was only mildly interested. He talked to anyone who would talk to him, though he was naturally a shy man. He talked to the barber, the grocer, the druggist, the streetcar conductor, the milkman, the iceman. But the price of wheat did not interest these gentlemen. They did not know that the price of wheat was the most vital topic of conversation in the world.

"Well, now," he would say, "you take this year's wheat crop, with about 917,000,000 bushels of wheat harvested, why, that's what's going to win the war! Yes, sirree! No wheat, no winning, that's what I say."

"Ya-as, it is!" the city men would scoff. But the queer part of it is that Farmer Ben was right.

Minnie got into the habit of using him as a sort of nursemaid. It gave her many hours of freedom for gadding and gossiping.

"Pa, will you look after Pearlie for a little while this morning? I got to run downtown to match something and she gets so tired and mean-acting if I take her along. Ma's going with me."

He loved the feel of Pearlie's small, velvet-soft hand in his big fist. He called her "little feller," and fed her forbidden dainties. His big brown fingers were miraculously deft at buttoning and unbuttoning her tiny garments, and wiping her soft lips, and performing a hundred tender offices. He was playing a sort of game with himself, pretending this was Dike become a baby again. Once the pair managed to get over to Lincoln Park, where they spent a glorious day looking at the animals, eating popcorn, and riding on the miniature railway.

They returned, tired, dusty, and happy, to a double tirade.

Bella engaged in a great deal of what she called worrying about Dike. Ben spoke of him seldom, but the boy was always present in his thoughts. They had written him of their move, but he had not seemed to get the impression of its permanence. His letters indicated that he thought they were visiting Minnie, or taking a vacation in the city. Dike's letters were few. Ben treasured them, and read and reread them. When the Armistice news came, and with it the possibility of Dike's return, Ben tried to fancy him fitting into the life of the city. And his whole being revolted at the thought.

He saw the pimply-faced, sallow youths standing at the corner of Halsted and Sixty-third, spitting languidly and handling their limp cigarettes with an amazing labial dexterity. Their conversation was low-voiced, sinister, and terse, and their eyes narrowed as they watched the overdressed, scarlet-lipped girls go by. A great fear clutched at Ben Westerveld's heart.

The lack of exercise and manual labor began to tell on Ben. He did not grow fat from idleness. Instead his skin seemed to sag and hang on his frame, like a garment grown too large for him. He walked a great deal. Perhaps that had something to do with it. He tramped miles of city pavements. He was a very lonely man. And then, one day, quite by accident, he came upon South Water Street. Came upon it, stared at it as a water-crazed traveler in a desert gazes upon the spring in the oasis, and drank from it, thirstily, gratefully.

South Water Street feeds Chicago. Into that close-packed thoroughfare come daily the fruits and vegetables that will supply a million tables. Ben had heard of it, vaguely, but had never attempted to find it. Now he stumbled upon it and, standing there, felt at home in Chicago for the first time in more than a year. He saw ruddy men walking about in overalls and carrying whips in their hands — wagon whips, actually. He hadn't seen men like that since he had left the farm. The sight of them sent a great pang of homesickness through him. His hand reached out and he ran an accustomed finger over the potatoes in a barrel on the walk. His fingers lingered and gripped them, and passed over them lovingly.

At the contact something within him that had been tight and hungry seemed to relax, satisfied. It was his nerves, feeding on those familiar things for which they had been starving.

He walked up one side and down the other. Crates of lettuce, bins of onions, barrels of apples. Such vegetables! The radishes were scarlet globes. Each carrot was a spear of pure orange. The green and purple of fancy asparagus held his expert eye. The cauliflower was like a great bouquet, fit for a bride; the cabbages glowed like jade.

And the men! He hadn't dreamed there were men

like that in this big, shiny-shod, stiffly laundered, white-collared city. Here were rufous men in overalls — worn, shabby, easy-looking overalls and old blue shirts, and mashed hats worn at a careless angle. Men, jovial, good-natured, with clear eyes, and having about them some of the revivifying freshness and wholesomeness of the products they handled.

Ben Westerveld breathed in the strong, pungent smell of onions and garlic and of the earth that seemed to cling to the vegetables, washed clean though they were. He breathed deeply, gratefully, and felt strangely at peace.

It was a busy street. A hundred times he had to step quickly to avoid a hand truck, or dray, or laden wagon. And yet the busy men found time to greet him friendlily. "H'are you!" they said genially. "H'are you this morning!"

He was marketwise enough to know that some of these busy people were commission men, and some grocers, and some buyers, stewards, clerks. It was a womanless thoroughfare. At the busiest business corner, though, in front of the largest commission house on the street, he saw a woman. Evidently she was transacting business, too, for he saw the men bringing boxes of berries and vegetables for her inspection. A woman in a plain blue skirt and a small black hat.

A funny job for a woman. What weren't they mixing into nowadays!

He turned sidewise in the narrow, crowded space in order to pass her little group. And one of the men — a red-cheeked, merry-looking young fellow in a white apron — laughed and said: "Well, Emma, you win. When it comes to driving a bargain with you, I quit. It can't be did!"

Even then he didn't know her. He did not dream that this straight, slim, tailored, white-haired woman, bargaining so shrewdly with these men, was the Emma Byers of the old days. But he stopped there a moment, in frank curiosity, and the woman looked up. She looked up, and he knew those intelligent eyes and that serene brow. He had carried the picture of them in his mind for more than thirty years, so it was not so surprising.

He did not hesitate. He might have if he had thought a moment, but he acted automatically. He stood before her. "You're Emma Byers, ain't you?"

She did not know him at first. Small blame to her, so completely had the roguish, vigorous boy vanished in this sallow, sad-eyed old man. Then: "Why, Ben!" she said quietly. And there was pity in her voice, though she did not mean to have it there. She put out one hand — that capable, reassuring hand — and gripped his and held it a moment. It was queer and significant that it should be his hand that lay within hers.

"Well, what in all get-out are you doing around here, Emma?" He tried to be jovial and easy. She turned to the aproned man with whom she had been dealing and smiled.

"What am I doing here, Joe?"

Joe grinned, waggishly. "Nothin'; only beatin' every man on the street at his own game, and makin' so much money that —"

But she stopped him there. "I guess I'll do my own explaining." She turned to Ben again. "And what are you doing here in Chicago?"

Ben passed a faltering hand across his chin. "Me? Well, I'm — we're living here, I s'pose. Livin' here."

She glanced at him sharply. "Left the farm, Ben?"
"Yes."

"Wait a minute." She concluded her business with Joe; finished it briskly and to her own satisfaction.

With her bright brown eyes and her alert manner and her quick little movements she made you think of a wren — a businesslike little wren — a very early wren that is highly versed in the worm-catching way.

At her next utterance he was startled but game.

"Have you had your lunch?"

"Why, no; I —"

"I've been down here since seven, and I'm starved. Let's go and have a bite at the little Greek restaurant around the corner. A cup of coffee and a sandwich, anyway."

Seated at the bare little table, she surveyed him with those intelligent, understanding, kindly eyes, and he felt the years slip from him. They were walking down the country road together, and she was listening quietly and advising him.

She interrogated him gently. But something of his old masterfulness came back to him. "No, I want to know about you first. I can't get the rights of it, you being here on South Water, tradin' and all."

So she told him briefly. She was in the commission business. Successful. She bought, too, for such hotels as the Blackstone and the Congress, and for half a dozen big restaurants. She gave him bare facts, but he was shrewd enough and sufficiently versed in business to know that here was a woman of established commercial position.

"But how does it happen you're keepin' it up, Emma, all this time? Why, you must be anyway — it ain't that you look it — but —" He floundered, stopped.

She laughed. "That's all right, Ben. I couldn't fool you on that. And I'm working because it keeps me happy. I want to work till I die. My children keep telling me to stop, but I know better than that. I'm not going to rust out. I want to wear out." Then, at an unspoken question in his eyes: "He's dead. These twenty years. It was hard at first, when the children were small. But I knew garden stuff if I didn't know anything else. It came natural to me. That's all."

So then she got his story from him bit by bit. He spoke of the farm and of Dike, and there was a great pride in his voice. He spoke of Bella, and the son who had been killed, and of Minnie. And the words came falteringly. He was trying to hide something, and he was not made for deception. When he had finished:

"Now, listen, Ben. You go back to your farm."

"I can't. She — I can't."

She leaned forward, earnestly. "You go back to the farm."

He turned up his palms with a little gesture of defeat. "I can't."

"You can't stay here. It's killing you. It's poisoning you. Did you ever hear of toxins? That means poisons, and you're poisoning yourself. You'll die of it. You've got another twenty years of work in you. What's ailing you? You go back to your wheat and your apples and your hogs. There isn't a bigger job in the world than that."

For a moment his face took on a glow from the warmth of her own inspiring personality. But it died again. When they rose to go, his shoulders drooped again, his muscles sagged. At the doorway he paused a moment, awkward in farewell. He blushed a little, stammered.

"Emma — I always wanted to tell you. God knows it was luck for you the way it turned out — but I always wanted to —"

She took his hand again in her firm grip at that, and her kindly, bright brown eyes were on him. "I never held it against you, Ben. I had to live a long time to understand it. But I never held a grudge. It just wasn't to be, I suppose. But listen to me, Ben. You do as I tell you. You go back to your wheat and your apples and your hogs. There isn't a bigger man-size job in the world. It's where you belong."

Unconsciously his shoulders straightened again. Again they sagged. And so they parted, the two.

He must have walked almost all the long way home, through miles and miles of city streets. He must have lost his way, too, for when he looked up at a corner street sign it was an unfamiliar one.

So he floundered about, asked his way, was misdirected. He took the right streetcar at last and got off at his own corner at seven o'clock, or later. He was in for a scolding, he knew.

But when he came to his own doorway he knew that even his tardiness could not justify the bedlam of sound that came from within. High-pitched voices. Bella's above all the rest, of course, but there was Minnie's too, and Gus's growl, and Pearlie's treble, and the boy Ed's and —

At the other voice his hand trembled so that the knob rattled in the door, and he could not turn it. But finally he did turn it, and stumbled in, breathing hard. And that other voice was Dike's.

He must have just arrived. The flurry of explanation was still in progress. Dike's knapsack was still on his back, and his canteen at his hip, his helmet slung over his shoulder. A brown, hard, glowing Dike, strangely tall and handsome and older, too. Older.

All this Ben saw in less than one electric second. Then he had the boy's two shoulders in his hands, and Dike was saying, "Hello, Pop."

Of the roomful, Dike and old Ben were the only quiet ones. The others were taking up the explanation and going over it again and again, and marveling, and asking questions.

"He come in to — what's that place, Dike? —

Hoboken — yesterday only. An' he sent a dispatch to the farm. Can't you read our letters, Dike, that you didn't know we was here now? And then he's only got an hour more. They got to go to Camp Grant to be, now, demobilized. He came out to Minnie's on a chance. Ain't he big!"

But Dike and his father were looking at each other quietly. Then Dike spoke. His speech was not phlegmatic, as of old. He had a new clipped way of uttering his words:

"Say, Pop, you ought to see the way the Frenchies farm! They got about an acre each, and, say, they use every inch of it. If they's a little dirt blows into the crotch of a tree, they plant a crop in there. I never seen nothin' like it. Say, we waste enough stuff over here to keep that whole country in food for a hundred years. Yessir. And tools! Outta the ark, believe me. If they ever saw our tractor, they'd think it was the Germans comin' back. But they're smart at that. I picked up a lot of new ideas over there. And you ought to see the old birds — womenfolks and men about eighty years old — runnin' everything on the farm. They had to. I learned somethin' off them about farmin'."

"Forget the farm," said Minnie.

"Yeh," echoed Gus, "forget the farm stuff. I can get you a job here out at the works for four-fifty a day, and six when you learn it right."

Dike looked from one to the other, alarm and unbelief on his face. "What d'you mean, a job? Who wants a job! What you all —"

Bella laughed jovially. "F'r heaven's sakes, Dike, wake up! We're livin' here. This is our place. We ain't rubes no more."

Dike turned to his father. A little stunned look crept into his face. A stricken, pitiful look. There was something about it that suddenly made old Ben think of

Pearlie when she had been slapped by her quick-tempered mother.

"But I been countin' on the farm," he said miserably. "I just been livin' on the idea of comin' back to it. Why, I — The streets here, they're all narrow and choked up. I been countin' on the farm. I want to go back and be a farmer. I want —"

And then Ben Westerveld spoke. A new Ben Westerveld — the old Ben Westerveld. Ben Westerveld, the farmer, the monarch over six hundred acres of bounteous bottomland.

"That's all right, Dike," he said. "You're going back. So'm I. I've got another twenty years of work in me. We're going back to the farm."

Bella turned on him, a wildcat. "We ain't! Not me! We ain't! I'm not agoin' back to the farm."

But Ben Westerveld was master again in his own house. "You're goin' back, Bella," he said quietly, "an' things are goin' to be different. You're goin' to run the house the way I say, or I'll know why. If you can't do it, I'll get them in that can. An' me and Dike, we're goin' back to our wheat and our apples and our hogs. Yessir! There ain't a bigger man-size job in the world."

Un Morso doo Pang

*W*hen you are twenty you do not patronize sunsets unless you are unhappy, in love, or both. Tessie Golden was both. Six months ago a sunset had wrung from her only a casual tribute, such as: "My! Look how red the sky is!" delivered as unemotionally as a weather bulletin.

Tessie Golden sat on the top step of the back porch now, a slim, inert heap in a cotton house coat and scuffed slippers. Her head was propped wearily against the porch post. Her hands were limp in her lap. Her face was turned toward the west, where shone that mingling of orange and rose known as salmon pink. But no answering radiance in the girl's face met the glow in the Wisconsin sky.

*S*aturday night, after supper in Chippewa, Wisconsin, Tessie Golden of the presunset era would have been calling from her bedroom to the kitchen: "Ma, what'd you do with my pink blouse?"

And from the kitchen: "It's in your second bureau drawer. The collar was kind of mussed from Wednesday night, and I give it a little pressing while my iron was on."

At seven-thirty Tessie would have emerged from her bedroom in the pink blouse that might have been considered alarmingly frank as to texture and precariously low as to neck had Tessie herself not been so reassuringly unopulent; a black taffeta skirt, very brief; a hat with a good deal of French blue about it; fragile high-heeled pumps with bows.

As she passed through the sitting room on her way out, her mother would appear in the doorway, dish-towel in hand. Her pride in this slim young thing and her love of her she concealed with a thin layer of carping criticism.

"Runnin' downtown again, I s'pose." A keen eye on the swishing skirt hem.

Tessie, the quick-tongued, would toss the wave of shining hair that lay against either glowing cheek. "Oh, my, no! I just thought I'd dress up in case Angie Hatton drove past in her auto and picked me up for a little ride. So's not to keep her waiting."

Angie Hatton was Old Man Hatton's daughter. Anyone in the Fox River Valley could have told you who Old Man Hatton was. You saw his name at the top of every letterhead of any importance in Chippewa, from the Pulp and Paper Mill to the First National Bank, and including the watch factory, the canning works, and the Mid-Western Land Company. Knowing this, you were able to appreciate Tessie's sarcasm. Angie Hatton was as unaware of Tessie's existence as only a young woman could be whose family residence was in Chippewa, Wisconsin, but who wintered in Italy, summered in the mountains, and bought (so the town said) her very hairpins in New York. When Angie Hatton came home from the East the town used to stroll past on Mondays to view the washing on the Hatton line. Angie's underwear, flirting so audaciously with the sunshine and zephyrs, was of silk and crepe de Chine and satin — materials that we had always thought of heretofore as intended exclusively for party dresses and wedding gowns. Of course, two years later they were showing practically the same thing at Megan's dry-goods store. But that was always the way with Angie Hatton. Even those of us who went to Chicago to shop never quite caught up with her.

Delivered of this ironic thrust, Tessie would walk toward the screen door with a little flaunting sway of the hips. Her mother's eyes, following the slim figure, had a sort of grudging love in them. A spare, caustic, wiry little woman, Tessie's mother. Tessie resembled her as a watercolor may resemble a blurred charcoal sketch. Tessie's wide mouth curved into humor lines. She was the cutup of the escapement department at the watch factory; the older woman's lips sagged at the corners. Tessie was buoyant and colorful with youth. The other was shrunken and faded with years and labor. As the girl minced across the room in her absurdly high-heeled shoes, the older woman thought: My, but she's pretty! But she said aloud: "I should think you'd stay home once in a while and not be runnin' the streets every night."

"Time enough to be sittin' home when I'm old like you."

And yet between these two there was love, and even understanding.

But in families such as Tessie's, demonstration is a thing to be ashamed of; affection a thing to conceal. Tessie's father was janitor of the Chippewa High School. A powerful man, slightly crippled by rheumatism, loquacious, lively, fond of his family, proud of

his neat gray frame house and his new cement sidewalk
and his carefully tended yard and garden patch. In all
her life Tessie had never seen a caress exchanged between her parents.

Nowadays Ma Golden had little occasion for finding
fault with Tessie's evening diversion. She no longer had
cause to say, "Always gaddin' downtown, or over to
Cora's or somewhere, like you didn't have a home to
stay in. You ain't been in a evening this week, only
when you washed your hair."

Tessie had developed a fondness for sunsets viewed
from the back porch — she who had thought nothing
of dancing until three and rising at half-past six to go
to work.

Stepping about in the kitchen after supper, her
mother would eye the limp, relaxed figure on the back
porch with a little pang at her heart. She would come
to the screen door, or even out to the porch on some
errand or other — to empty the coffee grounds, to turn
the row of half-ripe tomatoes reddening on the porch
railing, to flap and hang up a damp tea towel.

"Ain't you goin' out, Tess?"

"No."

"What you want to lop around here for? Such a grant
evening. Why don't you put on your things and run
downtown, or over to Cora's or somewhere, hm?"

"What for?" — listlessly.

"What for! What does anybody go out for!"

"I don't know."

If they could have talked it over together, these two,
the girl might have found relief. But the family shyness
of their class was too strong upon them. Once Mrs.
Golden had said, in an effort at sympathy, "Person'd
think Chuck Mory was the only one who'd gone to
war an' the last fella left in the world."

A grim flash of the old humor lifted the corners of

the wide mouth. "He is. Who's there left? Stumpy Gans, up at the railroad crossing? Or maybe Fatty Weiman, driving the garbage. Guess I'll doll up this evening and see if I can't make a hit with one of them."

She relapsed into bitter silence. The bottom had dropped out of Tessie Golden's world.

*I*n order to understand the Tessie of today one would have to know the Tessie of six months ago — Tessie the impudent, the life-loving. Tessie Golden could say things to the escapement-room foreman that anyone else would have been fired for. Her wide mouth was capable of glorious insolences. Whenever you heard shrieks of laughter from the girls' washroom at noon you knew that Tessie was holding forth to an admiring group. She was a born mimic; audacious, agile, and with the gift of burlesque. The autumn that Angie Hatton came home from Europe wearing the first tight skirt that Chippewa had ever seen, Tessie gave an imitation of that advanced young woman's progress down Grand Avenue in this restricting garment. The thing was cruel in its fidelity, though containing just enough exaggeration to make it artistic. She followed it up by imitating the stricken look on the face of Mattie Haynes, cloak-and-suit buyer at Megan's, who, having just returned from the East with what she considered the most fashionable of the new fall styles, now beheld Angie Hatton in the garb that was the last echo of the last cry in Paris modes — and no model in Mattie's newly selected stock bore even the remotest resemblance to it.

You would know from this that Tessie was not a particularly deft worker. Her big-knuckled fingers were cleverer at turning out a blouse or retrimming a hat.

Hers were what are known as handy hands, but not sensitive. It takes a light and facile set of fingers to fit pallet and arbor and fork together: close work and tedious. Seated on low benches along the tables, their chins almost level with the tabletop, the girls worked with pincers and flame, screwing together the three tiny parts of the watch's anatomy that were their particular specialty. Each wore a jeweler's glass in one eye. Tessie had worked at the watch factory for three years, and the pressure of the glass on the eye socket had given her the slightly hollow-eyed appearance peculiar to experienced watchmakers. It was not unbecoming, though, and lent her, somehow, a spiritual look which made her impudence all the more piquant.

Tessie wasn't always witty, really. But she had achieved a reputation for wit which insured applause for even her feebler efforts. Nap Ballou, the foreman, never left the escapement room without a little shiver of nervous apprehension — a feeling justified by the ripple of suppressed laughter that went up and down the long tables. He knew that Tessie Golden, like a naughty schoolgirl when teacher's back is turned, had directed one of her sure shafts at him.

Ballou, his face darkling, could easily have punished her. Tessie knew it. But he never did, or would. She knew that, too. Her very insolence and audacity saved her.

"Someday," Ballou would warn her, "you'll get too gay, and then you'll find yourself looking for a job."

"Go on — fire me," retorted Tessie, "and I'll meet you in Lancaster" — a form of wit appreciated only by watchmakers. For there is a certain type of watch hand who is as peripatetic as the old-time printer. Restless, ne'er-do-well, spendthrift, he wanders from factory to factory through the chain of watch-making towns: Springfield, Trenton, Waltham, Lancaster, Waterbury,

Chippewa. Usually expert, always unreliable, certainly fond of drink, Nap Ballou was typical of his kind. The steady worker had a mingled admiration and contempt for him. He, in turn, regarded the other as a stick-in-the-mud. Nap wore his cap on one side of his curly head, and drank so evenly and steadily as never to be quite drunk and never strictly sober. He had slender, sensitive fingers like an artist's or a woman's, and he knew the parts of that intricate mechanism known as a watch from the jewel to the finishing room. It was said he had a wife or two. He was forty-six, good-looking in a dissolute sort of way, possessing the charm of the wanderer, generous with his money. It was known that Tessie's barbs were permitted to prick him without retaliation because Tessie herself appealed to his errant fancy.

When the other girls teased her about this obvious state of affairs, something fine and contemptuous welled up in her. "Him! Why, say, he ought to work in a pickle factory instead of a watchworks. All he needs is a little dill and a handful of grape leaves to make him good eatin' as a relish."

And she thought of Chuck Mory, perched on the high seat of the American Express truck, hatless, sunburned, stockily muscular, clattering down Winnebago Street on his way to the depot and the 7:50 train.

Something about the clear simplicity and uprightness of the firm little figure appealed to Nap Ballou. He used to regard her curiously with a long, hard gaze before which she would grow uncomfortable. "Think you'll know me next time you see me?" But there was an uneasy feeling beneath her flip exterior. Not that there was anything of the beautiful, persecuted factory girl and villainous foreman about the situation. Tessie worked at watch-making because it was light, pleasant, and well paid. She could have found another job for the asking. Her money went for shoes and blouses and lingerie and silk stockings. She was forever buying a vivid necktie for her father and dressing up her protesting mother in gay colors that went ill with the drab, wrinkled face. "If it wasn't for me, you'd go round looking like one of those Polack women down by the tracks," Tessie would scold. "It's a wonder you don't wear a shawl!"

That was the Tessie of six months ago, gay, carefree, holding the reins of her life in her own two capable hands. Three nights a week, and Sunday, she saw Chuck Mory. When she went downtown on Saturday night it was frankly to meet Chuck, who was waiting for her on Schroeder's drugstore corner. He knew it, and she knew it. Yet they always went through a little ceremony. She and Cora, turning into Grand from Winnebago Street, would make for the post office. Then down the length of Grand with a leaping glance at Schroeder's corner before they reached it. Yes, there they were, very clean-shaven, clean-shirted, slick-looking. Tessie would have known Chuck's blond head among a thousand. An air of studied hauteur and indifference as they approached the corner. Heads turned the other way. A low whistle from the boys.

"Oh, how do!"

"Good evening!"

Both greetings done with careful surprise. Then on down the street. On the way back you took the inside of the walk, and your hauteur was now stony to the point of insult. Schroeder's corner simply did not exist. On as far as Megan's, which you entered and inspected, up one brightly lighted aisle and down the next. At the dress-goods counter there was a neat little stack of pamphlets entitled "In the World of Fashion." You took one and sauntered out leisurely. Down Winnebago Street now, homeward bound, talking animatedly and seemingly unconscious of quick footsteps sounding nearer and nearer. Just past the Burke House, where the residential district began, and where the trees cast their kindly shadows: "Can I see you home?" A hand slipped through her arm; a little tingling thrill.

"Oh, why, how do, Chuck! Hello, Scotty. Sure, if you're going our way."

At every turn Chuck left her side and dashed around behind her in order to place himself at her right again, according to the rigid rule of Chippewa etiquette. He took her arm only at street crossings until they reached the tracks, which perilous spot seemed to justify him in retaining his hold throughout the remainder of the stroll. Usually they lost Cora and Scotty without having been conscious of their loss.

Their talk? The girls and boys that each knew; the day's happenings at factory and express office; next Wednesday night's dance up in the Chute; and always the possibility of Chuck's leaving the truck and assuming the managership of the office.

"Don't let this go any further, see? But I heard it straight that old Benke is going to be transferred to Fond du Lac. And if he is, why, I step in, see? Benke's got a girl in Fondy, and he's been pluggin' to get there. Gee, maybe I won't be glad when he does!" A little silence. "Will you be glad, Tess? Hm?"

Tess felt herself glowing and shivering as the big hand closed more tightly on her arm. "Me? Why, sure I'll be pleased to see you get a job that's coming to you by rights, and that'll get you better pay, and all."

But she knew what he meant, and he knew she knew.

No more of that now. Chuck — gone. Scotty — gone. All the boys at the watchworks, all the fellows in the neighborhood — gone. At first she hadn't minded. It was exciting. You kidded them at first: "Well, believe me, Chuck, if you shoot the way you play ball, you're a gone goon already."

"All you got to do, Scotty, is to stick that face of yours up over the top of the trench and the Germans'll die of fright and save you wasting bullets."

There was a great knitting of socks and sweaters and caps. Tessie's big-knuckled, capable fingers made you dizzy, they flew so fast. Chuck was outfitted as for a polar expedition. Tess took half a day off to bid him good-bye. They marched down Grand Avenue, that first lot of them, in their everyday suits and hats, with their shiny yellow suitcases and their pasteboard boxes in their hands, sheepish, red-faced, awkward. In their eyes, though, a certain look. And so off for Camp Sherman, their young heads sticking out of the car windows in clusters — black, yellow, brown, red. But for each woman on the depot platform there was just one head. Tessie saw a blurred blond one with a misty halo around it. A great shouting and waving of hand-kerchiefs:

"Good-bye! Good-bye! Write, now! Be sure! Mebbe you can get off in a week, for a visit. Good-bye! Good —"

They were gone. Their voices came back to the crowd on the depot platform — high, clear young voices; almost like the voices of children, shouting.

Well, you wrote letters — fat, bulging letters — and in turn you received equally plump envelopes with a red emblem in one corner.

You sent boxes of homemade fudge (nut variety) and cookies and the more durable forms of cake.

Then, unaccountably, Chuck was whisked all the way to California.

He was furious at parting with his mates, and his indignation was expressed in his letters to Tessie. She sympathized with him in her replies. She tried to make light of it, but there was a little clutch of terror in it, too. California! Might as well send a person to the end of the world while they were about it. Two months of that. Then, inexplicably again, Chuck's letters bore the astounding postmark of New York. She thought, in a panic, that he was Franceward bound, but it turned out not to be so. Not yet. Chuck's letters were taking on a cosmopolitan tone. "Well," he wrote, "I guess the little old town is as dead as ever. It seems funny you being right there all this time and I've traveled from the Atlantic to the Pacific. Everybody treats me swell. You ought to seen some of those California houses. They make Hatton's place look like a dump."

The girls, Cora and Tess and the rest, laughed and joked among themselves and assured one another, with a toss of the head, that they could have a good time without the fellas. They didn't need boys around.

They gave parties, and they were not a success. There was one of the type known as a stag. "Some hen party!" they all said. They danced, and sang "Over There." They had ice cream and chocolate layer cake and went home in great hilarity, with their hands on each other's shoulders, still singing.

But the thing was a failure, and they knew it. Next day, at the lunch hour and in the washroom, there was a little desultory talk about the stag. But the meat of such an after-gathering is contained in phrases such as "I says to him" — and "He says to me." They wasted little conversation on the stag. It was much more exciting to exhibit letters on blue-lined paper with the red emblem at the top. Chuck's last letter had contained the news of his sergeancy.

Angie Hatton, home from the East, was writing letters, too. Everyone in Chippewa knew that. She wrote on that new art paper with the gnawed-looking edges and stiff as a newly laundered cuff. But the letters which she awaited so eagerly were written on the same

sort of paper as were those Tessie had from Chuck —
blue-lined, cheap in quality. A New York fellow, Chippewa learned; an aviator. They knew, too, that young
Hatton was an infantry lieutenant somewhere in the
East. These letters were not from him.

Ever since her home-coming, Angie had been sewing
at the Red Cross shop on Grand Avenue. Chippewa
boasted two Red Cross shops. The Grand Avenue shop
was the society shop. The East End crowd sewed there,
capped, veiled, aproned — and unapproachable. Were
your fingers ever so deft, your knowledge of seams and
basting mathematical, your skill with that complicated
garment known as a pneumonia jacket uncanny, if you
did not belong to the East End set, you did not sew at
the Grand Avenue shop. No matter how grossly red
the blood which the Grand Avenue bandages and pads
were ultimately to stanch, the liquid in the fingers that
rolled and folded them was pure cerulean.

Tessie and her crowd had never thought of giving
any such service to their country. They spoke of the
Grand Avenue workers as "that stinkin' bunch." Yet
each one of the girls was capable of starting a blouse
in an emergency on Saturday night and finishing it in
time for a Sunday picnic, buttonholes and all. Their
help might have been invaluable. It never was asked.

Without warning, Chuck came home on three days'
furlough. It meant that he was bound for France right
enough this time. But Tessie didn't care.

"I don't care where you're goin'," she said exultantly,
her eyes lingering on the stocky, straight, powerful
figure in its rather ill-fitting khaki. "You're here now.
That's enough. Ain't you tickled to be home, Chuck?
Gee!"

"I'll say," responded Chuck. But even he seemed to
detect some lack in his tone and words. He elaborated
somewhat shamefacedly:

"Sure. It's swell to be home. But I don't know. After you've traveled around, and come back, things look so kind of little to you. I don't know — kind of —" He floundered about, at a loss for expression. Then tried again: "Now, take Hatton's place, for example. I always used to think it was a regular palace, but, gosh, you ought to see places where I was asked to in San Francisco and around there. Why, they was — were — enough to make the Hatton house look like a shack. Swimmin' pools of white marble, and acres of yard like a park, and the help always bringing you something to eat or drink. And the folks themselves — why, say! Here we are scraping and bowing to Hattons and that bunch. They're pikers to what some people are that invited me to their houses in New York and Berkeley, and treated me and the other guys like kings or something. Take Megan's store, too" — he was warming to his subject, so that he failed to notice the darkening of Tessie's face — "it's a joke compared to New York and San Francisco stores. Reg'lar hick joint."

Tessie stiffened. Her teeth were set, her eyes sparkled. She tossed her head. "Well, I'm sure, Mr. Mory, it's good enough for me. Too bad you had to come home at all now you're so elegant and swell, and everything. You better go call on Angie Hatton instead of wasting time on me. She'd probably be tickled to see you."

He stumbled to his feet, then, awkwardly. "Aw, say, Tessie, I didn't mean — why, say — you don't suppose — why, believe me, I pretty near busted out cryin' when I saw the Junction eatin' house when my train came in. And I been thinking of you every minute. There wasn't a day —"

"Tell that to your swell New York friends. I may be a hick but I ain't a fool." She was near to tears.

"Why, say, Tess, listen! Listen! If you knew — if you knew — A guy's got to — he's got no right to —"

And presently Tessie was mollified, but only on the surface. She smiled and glanced and teased and sparkled. And beneath was terror. He talked differently. He walked differently. It wasn't his clothes or the army. It was something else — an ease of manner, a new leisureliness of glance, an air. Once Tessie had gone to Milwaukee over Labor Day. It was the extent of her experience as a traveler. She remembered how superior she had felt for at least two days after. But Chuck! California! New York! It wasn't the distance that terrified her. It was his new knowledge, the broadening of his vision, though she did not know it and certainly could not have put it into words.

They went walking down by the river to Oneida Springs, and drank some of the sulfur water that tasted like rotten eggs. Tessie drank it with little shrieks and shudders and puckered her face up into an expression indicative of extreme disgust.

"It's good for you," Chuck said, and drank three cups of it, manfully. "That taste is the mineral qualities the water contains — sulfur and iron and so forth."

"I don't care," snapped Tessie irritably. "I hate it!" They had often walked along the river and tasted of the spring water, but Chuck had never before waxed scientific. They took a boat at Baumann's boathouse and drifted down the lovely Fox River.

"Want to row?" Chuck asked. "I'll get an extra pair of oars if you do."

"I don't know how. Besides, it's too much work. I guess I'll let you do it."

Chuck was fitting his oars in the oarlocks. She stood on the landing looking down at him. His hat was off. His hair seemed blonder than ever against the rich tan of his face. His neck muscles swelled a little as he bent. Tessie felt a great longing to bury her face in the warm red skin. He straightened with a sigh and smiled at her.

"I'll be ready in a minute." He took off his coat and turned his khaki shirt in at the throat, so that you saw the white line of his untanned chest in strange contrast to his sun-burned throat. A feeling of giddy faintness surged over Tessie. She stepped blindly into the boat and would have fallen if Chuck's hard, firm grip had not steadied her. "Whoa, there! Don't you know how to step into a boat? There. Walk along the middle."

She sat down and smiled up at him. "I don't know how I come to do that. I never did before."

Chuck braced his feet, rolled up his sleeves, and took an oar in each brown hand, bending rhythmically to his task. He looked about him, then at the girl, and drew a deep breath, feathering his oars. "I guess I must have dreamed about this more'n a million times."

"Have you, Chuck?"

They drifted on in silence. "Say, Tess, you ought to learn to row. It's good exercise. Those girls in California and New York, they play tennis and row and swim as good as the boys. Honest, some of 'em are wonders!"

Oh, I'm sick of your swell New York friends! Can't you talk about something else?"

He saw that he had blundered without in the least understanding how or why. "All right. What'll we talk about?" In itself a fatal admission.

"About — you." Tessie made it a caress.

"Me? Nothin' to tell about me. I just been drillin' and studyin' and marchin' and readin' some — Oh, say, what d'you think?"

"What?"

"They been learnin' us — teachin' us, I mean — French. It's the darnedest language! Bread is pain. Can you beat that? If you want to ask for a piece of bread, you say like this: *Donnay ma un morso doo pang.* See?"

"My!" breathed Tessie.

And within her something was screaming: Oh, my

God! Oh, my God! He knows French. And those girls that can row and swim and everything. And me, I don't know anything. Oh, God, what'll I do?

It was as though she could see him slipping away from her, out of her grasp, out of her sight. She had no fear of what might come to him in France. Bullets and bayonets would never hurt Chuck. He'd make it, just as he always made the 7:50 when it seemed as if he was going to miss it sure. He'd make it there and back, all right. But he'd be a different Chuck, while she stayed the same Tessie. Books, travel, French, girls, swell folks —

And all the while she was smiling and dimpling and trailing her hand in the water. "Bet you can't guess what I got in that lunch box."

"Chocolate cake."

"Well, of course I've got chocolate cake. I baked it myself this morning."

"Yes, you did!" "Why, Chuck Mory, I did so! I guess you think I can't do anything, the way you talk."

"Oh, don't I! I guess you know what I think."

"Well, it isn't the cake I mean. It's something else."

"Fried chicken!"

"Oh, now you've gone and guessed it." She pouted prettily.

"You asked me to, didn't you?"

Then they laughed together, as at something exquisitely witty. Down the river, drifting, rowing. Tessie pointed to a house half hidden among the trees on the farther shore: "There's Hatton's camp. They say they have grand times there with their swell crowd some Saturdays and Sundays. If I had a house like that, I'd live in it all the time, not just a couple of days out of the whole year." She hesitated a moment. "I suppose it looks like a shanty to you now."

Chuck surveyed it, patronizingly. "No, it's a nice

little place."

They beached their boat, and built a little fire, and had supper on the riverbank, and Tessie picked out the choice bits for him — the breast of the chicken, beautifully golden brown; the ripest tomato; the firmest, juiciest pickle; the corner of the little cake which would give him a double share of icing.

From Chuck, between mouthfuls: "I guess you don't know how good this tastes. Camp grub's all right, but after you've had a few months of it you get so you don't believe there *is* such a thing as real fried chicken and homemade chocolate cake."

"I'm glad you like it, Chuck. Here, take this drumstick. You ain't eating a thing!" His fourth piece of chicken.

Down the river as far as the danger line just above the dam, with Tessie pretending fear just for the joy of having Chuck reassure her. Then back again in the dusk, Chuck bending to the task now against the current. And so up the hill, homeward bound. They walked very slowly, Chuck's hand on her arm. They were dumb with the tragic, eloquent dumbness of their kind. If she could have spoken the words that were churning in her mind, they would have been something like this:

"Oh, Chuck, I wish I was married to you. I wouldn't care if only I had you. I wouldn't mind babies or anything. I'd be glad. I want our house, with a dining room set, and a mahogany bed, and one of those overstuffed sets in the living room, and all the housework to do. I'm scared. I'm scared I won't get it. What'll I do if I don't?"

And he, wordlessly: "Will you wait for me, Tessie, and keep on thinking about me? And will you keep yourself like you are so that if I come back —"

Aloud, she said: "I guess you'll get stuck on one of

those French girls. I should worry! They say wages at the watch factory are going to be raised, workers are so scarce. I'll probably be as rich as Angie Hatton time you get back."

And he, miserably: "Little old Chippewa girls are good enough for Chuck. I ain't counting on taking up with those Frenchies. I don't like their jabber, from what I know of it. I saw some pictures of 'em, last week, a fellow in camp had who'd been over there. Their hair is all funny, and fixed up with combs and stuff, and they look real dark like foreigners."

It had been reassuring enough at the time. But that was six months ago. And now here was the Tessie who sat on the back porch, evenings, surveying the sunset. A listless, lackadaisical, brooding Tessie. Little point to going downtown Saturday nights now. There was no familiar, beloved figure to follow you swiftly as you turned off Elm Street, homeward bound. If she went downtown now, she saw only those Saturday-night family groups which are familiar to every small town. The husband, very damp as to hair and clean as to shirt, guarding the go-cart outside while the woman accomplished her Saturday-night trading at Ding's or Halpin's. Sometimes there were as many as half a dozen go-carts outside Halpin's, each containing a sleeping burden, relaxed, chubby, fat-cheeked. The waiting men smoked their pipes and conversed largely. "Hello, Ed. The woman's inside, buyin' the store out, I guess."

"That so? Mine, to. Well, how's everything?"

Tessie knew that presently the woman would come out, bundle laden, and that she would stow these lesser bundles in every corner left available by the more important sleeping bundle — two yards of oilcloth; a spool of 100, white; a banana for the baby; a new stew pan at the five-and-ten.

There had been a time when Tessie, if she thought

of these women at all, felt sorry for them — worn, drab, lacking in style and figure. Now she envied them.

*T*here were weeks upon weeks when no letter came from Chuck. In his last letter there had been some talk of his being sent to Russia. Tessie's eyes, large enough now in her thin face, distended with a great fear. Russia! His letter spoke, too, of French villages and chateaux. He and a bunch of fellows had been introduced to a princess or a countess or something — it was all one to Tessie — and what do you think? She had kissed them all on both cheeks! Seems that's the way they did in France.

The morning after the receipt of this letter the girls at the watch factory might have remarked her pallor had they not been so occupied with a new and more absorbing topic.

"Tess, did you hear about Angie Hatton?"

"What about her?"

"She's going to France. It's in the Milwaukee paper, all about her being Chippewa's fairest daughter, and a picture of the house, and her being the belle of the Fox River Valley, and she's giving up her palatial home and all to go to work in a canteen for her country and bleeding France."

"Ya-as she is!" sneered Tessie, and a dull red flush, so deep as to be painful, swept over her face from throat to brow. "Ya-as she is, the doll-faced simp! Why, say, she never wiped up a floor in her life, or baked a cake, or stood on them feet of hers. She couldn't cut up a loaf of bread decent. Bleeding France! Ha! That's rich, that is." She thrust her chin out brutally, and her eyes narrowed to slits. "She's going over there after that fella of hers. She's chasing him. It's now or never, and she knows it and she's scared, same's the rest of us. On'y we got to set home and make the best of it. Or take what's left." She turned her head slowly to where Nap Ballou stood over a table at the far end of the room. She laughed a grim, unlovely little laugh. "I guess when you can't go after what you want, like Angie, why you gotta take second choice."

All that day, at the bench, she was the reckless, insolent, audacious Tessie of six months ago. Nap Ballou was always standing over her, pretending to inspect some bit of work or other, his shoulder brushing hers. She laughed up at him so that her face was not more than two inches from his. He flushed, but she did not. She laughed a reckless little laugh.

"Thanks for helping teach me my trade, Mr. Ballou. 'Course I only been at it over three years now, so I ain't got the hang of it yet."

He straightened up slowly, and as he did so he rested a hand on her shoulder for a brief moment. She did not shrug it off.

*T*hat night, after supper, Tessie put on her hat and strolled down to Park Avenue. It wasn't for the walk. Tessie had never been told to exercise systematically for her body's good, or her mind's. She went in a spirit of unwholesome brooding curiosity and a bitter resentment. Going to France, was she? Lots of good she'd do there. Better stay home and — and what? Tessie cast about in her mind for a fitting job for Angie. Guess she might's well go, after all. Nobody'd miss her, unless it was her father, and he didn't see her but about a third of the time. But in Tessie's heart was a great envy of this girl who could bridge the hideous waste of ocean that separated her from her man. Bleeding

France. Yeh! Joke!

The Hatton place, built and landscaped twenty years before, occupied a square block in solitary grandeur, the show place of Chippewa. In architectural style it was an impartial mixture of Norman castle, French chateau, and Rhenish schloss, with a dash of Coney Island about its façade. It represented Old Man Hatton's realized dream of landed magnificence.

Tessie, walking slowly past it, and peering through the high iron fence, could not help noting an air of unwonted excitement about the place, usually so aloof, so coldly serene. Automobiles standing out in front. People going up and down. They didn't look very cheerful. Just as if it mattered whether anything happened to her or not!

Tessie walked around the block and stood a moment, uncertainly. Then she struck off down Grand Avenue and past Donovan's pool shack. A little group of after-supper idlers stood outside, smoking and gossiping, as she knew there would be. As she turned the corner she saw Nap Ballou among them. She had known that, too. As she passed she looked straight ahead, without bowing. But just past the Burke House he caught up with her. No half-shy "Can I walk home with you?" from Nap Ballou. No. Instead: "Hello, sweetheart!"

"Hello, yourself."

"Somebody's looking mighty pretty this evening, all dolled up in pink."

"Think so?" She tried to be pertly indifferent, but it was good to have someone following, someone walking home with you. What if he was old enough to be her father, with graying hair? Lots of the movie heroes had graying hair at the sides.

They walked for an hour. Tessie left him at the corner. She had once heard her father designate Ballou as "that drunken skunk." When she entered the sitting room her cheeks held an unwonted pink. Her eyes were brighter than they had been in months. Her mother looked up quickly, peering at her over a pair of steel-rimmed spectacles, very much askew.

"Where you been, Tessie?"

"Oh, walkin'."

"Who with?"

"Cora."

"Why, she was here, callin' for you, not more'n an hour ago."

Tessie, taking off her hat on her way upstairs, met this coolly. "Yeh, I ran into her comin' back."

Upstairs, lying fully dressed on her hard little bed, she stared up into the darkness, thinking, her hands limp at her sides. Oh, well, what's the diff? You had to make the best of it. Everybody makin' a fuss about the soldiers — feeding 'em, and asking 'em to their houses, and sending 'em things, and giving dances and picnics and parties so they wouldn't be lonesome. Chuck had told her all about it. The other boys told the same. They could just pick and choose their good times. Tessie's mind groped about, sensing a certain injustice. How about the girls? She didn't put it thus squarely. Hers was not a logical mind. Easy enough to paw over the menfolks and get silly over brass buttons and a uniform. She put it that way. She thought of the refrain of a popular song: "What Are You Going to Do to Help the Boys?" Tessie, smiling a crooked little smile up there in the darkness, parodied the words deftly: "What're you going to do to help the girls?" she demanded. "What're you going to do —" She rolled over on one side and buried her head in her arms.

*T*here was news again next morning at the watch factory. Tessie of the old days had never needed to depend on the other girls for the latest bit of gossip. Her alert eye and quick ear had always caught it first. But of late she had led a cloistered existence, indifferent to the world about her. The *Chippewa Courier* went into the newspaper pile behind the kitchen door without a glance from Tessie's incurious eye.

She was late this morning. As she sat down at the bench and fitted her glass in her eye, the chatter of the others, pitched in the high key of unusual excitement, penetrated even her listlessness.

"And they say she never screeched or fainted or anything. She stood there, kind of quiet, looking straight ahead, and then all of a sudden she ran to her pa —"

"I feel sorry for her. She never did anything to me. She —"

Tessie spoke, her voice penetrating the staccato fragments all about her and gathering them into a whole. "Say, who's the heroine of this picture? I come in in the middle of the film, I guess."

They turned on her with the unlovely eagerness of those who have ugly news to tell. They all spoke at once, in short sentences, their voices high with the note of hysteria.

"Angie Hatton's beau was killed —"

"They say his airyoplane fell ten thousand feet —"

"The news come only last evening about eight —"

"She won't see nobody but her pa —"

Eight! At eight Tessie had been standing outside Hatton's house, envying Angie and hating her. So that explained the people, and the automobiles, and the excitement. Tessie was not receiving the news with the dramatic reaction which its purveyors felt it deserved.

Tessie, turning from one to the other quietly, had said nothing. She was pitying Angie. Oh, the luxury of it! Nap Ballou, coming in swiftly to still the unwonted commotion in work hours, found Tessie the only one quietly occupied in that chatter-filled room. She was smiling as she worked. Nap Ballou, bending over her on some pretense that deceived no one, spoke low-voiced in her ear. But she veiled her eyes insolently and did not glance up. She hummed contentedly all the morning at her tedious work.

She had promised Nap Ballou to go picnicking with him Sunday. Down the river, boating, with supper on shore. The small, still voice within her had said, "Don't go! Don't go!" But the harsh, high-pitched, reckless overtone said, "Go on! Have a good time. Take all you can get."

She would have to lie at home and she did it. Some fabrication about the girls at the watchworks did the trick. Fried chicken, chocolate cake. She packed them deftly and daintily. High-heeled shoes, flimsy blouse, rustling skirt. Nap Ballou was waiting for her over in the city park. She saw him before he espied her. He was leaning against a tree, idly, staring straight ahead with queer, lackluster eyes. Silhouetted there against the tender green of the pretty square, he looked very old, somehow, and different — much older than he looked in his shop clothes, issuing orders. Tessie noticed that he sagged where he should have stuck out, and protruded where he should have been flat. There flashed across her mind a vividly clear picture of Chuck as she had last seen him — brown, fit, high of chest, flat of stomach, slim of flank.

Ballou saw her. He straightened and came toward her swiftly. "Somebody looks mighty sweet this afternoon."

Tessie plumped the heavy lunch box into his arms.

"When you get a line you like you stick to it, don't you?"

Down at the boathouse even Tessie, who had confessed ignorance of boats and oars, knew that Ballou was fumbling clumsily. He stooped to adjust the oars to the oarlocks. His hat was off. His hair looked very gray in the cruel spring sunshine. He straightened and smiled up at her.

"Ready in a minute, sweetheart," he said. He took off his collar and turned in the neckband of his shirt. His skin was very white. Tessie felt a little shudder of disgust sweep over her, so that she stumbled a little as she stepped into the boat.

The river was very lovely. Tessie trailed her fingers in the water and told herself that she was having a grand time. She told Nap the same when he asked her.

"Having a good time, little beauty?" he said. He was puffing a little with the unwonted exercise.

Tessie tried some of her old-time pertness of speech. "Oh, good enough, considering the company."

He laughed admiringly at that and said she was a sketch.

When the early evening came on they made a clumsy landing and had supper. This time Nap fed her the tidbits, though she protested.

"White meat for you," he said, "with your skin like milk."

"You must of read that in a book," scoffed Tessie. She glanced around her at the deepening shadows. "We haven't got much time.

It gets dark so early."

"No hurry," Nap assured her. He went on eating in a leisurely, finicking sort of way, though he consumed very little food, actually.

"You're not eating much," Tessie said once, halfheartedly. She decided that she wasn't having such a very grand time, after all, and that she hated his teeth, which were very bad. Now, Chuck's strong, white, double row —

"Well," she said, "let's be going."

"No hurry," again.

Tessie looked up at that with the instinctive fear of her kind. "What d'you mean, no hurry! 'Spect to stay here till dark?" She laughed at her own joke.

"Yes."

She got up then, the blood in her face. "Well, *I* don't."

He rose, too. "Why not?"

"Because I don't, that's why." She stooped and began picking up the remnants of the lunch, placing spoons and glass bottles swiftly and thriftily into the lunch box. Nap stepped around behind her.

"Let me help," he said. And then his arm was about her and his face was close to hers, and Tessie did not like it. He kissed her after a little wordless struggle. And then she knew. She had been kissed before. But not like this. Not like this! She struck at him furiously. Across her mind flashed the memory of a girl who had worked in the finishing room. A nice girl, too. But that hadn't helped her. Nap Ballou was laughing a little as he clasped her.

At that she heard herself saying: "I'll get Chuck Mory after you — you drunken bum, you! He'll lick you black and blue. He'll —"

The face, with the ugly, broken brown teeth, was coming close again. With all the young strength that was in her she freed one hand and clawed at that face from eyes to chin. A howl of pain rewarded her. His hold loosened. Like a flash she was off. She ran. It seemed to her that her feet did not touch the earth. Over brush, through bushes, crashing against trees, on and on. She heard him following her, but the broken-down engine that was his heart refused to do the work. She ran on, though her fear was as great as before. Fear of what might have happened — to her, Tessie Golden, that nobody could even talk fresh to. She gave a sob of fury and fatigue. She was stumbling now. It was growing dark. She ran on again, in fear of the overtaking darkness. It was easier now. Not so many trees and bushes. She came to a fence, climbed over it, lurched as she landed, leaned against it weakly for support, one hand on her aching heart. Before her was the Hatton summer cottage, dimly outlined in the twilight among the trees.

A warm, flickering light danced in the window. Tessie stood a moment, breathing painfully, sobbingly. Then, with an instinctive gesture, she patted her hair, tidied her blouse, and walked uncertainly toward the house, up the steps to the door. She stood there a moment, swaying slightly. Somebody'd be there.

The light. The woman who cooked for them or the man who took care of the place. Somebody'd —

She knocked at the door feebly. She'd tell 'em she had lost her way and got scared when it began to get dark. She knocked again, louder now. Footsteps. She braced herself and even arranged a crooked smile. The door opened wide. Old Man Hatton!

She looked up at him, terror and relief in her face. He peered over his glasses at her. "Who is it?" Tessie had not known, somehow, that his face was so kindly.

Tessie's carefully planned story crumbled into nothingness. "It's me!" she whimpered. "It's me!"

He reached out and put a hand on her arm and drew her inside.

"Angie! Angie! Here's a poor little kid —"

Tessie clutched frantically at the last crumbs of her pride. She tried to straighten, to smile with her old bravado. What was that story she had planned to tell?

"Who is it, Dad? Who — ?" Angie Hatton came into the hallway. She stared at Tessie. Then: "Why, my dear!" she said. "My dear! Come in here."

Angie Hatton! Tessie began to cry weakly, her face buried in Angie Hatton's expensive shoulder. Tessie remembered later that she had felt no surprise at the act.

"There, there!" Angie Hatton was saying. "Just poke up the fire, Dad. And get something from the dining room. Oh, I don't know. To drink, you know. Something —"

Then Old Man Hatton stood over her, holding a small glass to her lips. Tessie drank it obediently, made a wry little face, coughed, wiped her eyes, and sat up. She looked from one to the other, like a trapped little animal. She put a hand to her tousled head.

"That's all right," Angie Hatton assured her. "You can fix it after a while."

There they were, the three of them: Old Man Hatton with his back to the fire, looking benignly down upon her; Angie seated, with some knitting in her hands, as if entertaining bedraggled, tear-stained young ladies at dusk were an everyday occurrence; Tessie, twisting her handkerchief in a torment of embarrassment. But they asked no questions, these two. They evinced no curiosity about this disheveled creature who had flung herself in upon their decent solitude.

Tessie stared at the fire. She looked up at Old Man Hatton's face and opened her lips. She looked down and shut them again. Then she flashed a quick look at Angie, to see if she could detect there some suspicion, some disdain. None. Angie Hatton looked — well, Tessie put it to herself, thus: "She looks like she'd cried till she couldn't cry no more — only inside."

And then, surprisingly, Tessie began to talk. "I wouldn't never have gone with this fella, only Chuck, he was gone. All the boys're gone. It's fierce. You get scared, sitting home, waiting, and they're in France and everywhere, learning French and everything, and meeting grand people and having a fuss made over 'em. So I got mad and said I didn't care, I wasn't going to squat home all my life, waiting —"

Angie Hatton had stopped knitting now. Old Man Hatton was looking down at her very kindly. And so Tessie went on. The pent-up emotions and thoughts of these past months were finding an outlet at last. These things which she had never been able to discuss with her mother she now was laying bare to Angie Hatton and Old Man Hatton! They asked no questions. They seemed to understand. Once Old Man Hatton interrupted with: "So that's the kind of fellow they've got as escapement-room foreman, eh?"

Tessie, whose mind was working very clearly now, put out a quick hand. "Say, it wasn't his fault. He's a bum, all right, but I knew it, didn't I? It was me. I didn't care. Seemed to me it didn't make no difference who I went with, but it does." She looked down at her hands clasped so tightly in her lap.

"Yes, it makes a whole lot of difference," Angie agreed, and looked up at her father.

At that Tessie blurted her last desperate problem: "He's learning all kind of new things. Me, I ain't learning anything. When Chuck comes home he'll just think I'm dumb, that's all. He —"

"What kind of thing would you like to learn, Tessie, so that when Chuck comes home —"

Tessie looked up then, her wide mouth quivering with eagerness. "I'd like to learn to swim — and row a boat — and play tennis — like the rich girls — like the girls that's making such a fuss over the soldiers."

Angie Hatton was not laughing. So, after a moment's hesitation, Tessie brought out the worst of it. "And French. I'd like to learn to talk French."

Old Man Hatton had been surveying his shoes, his mouth grim. He looked at Angie now and smiled a little. "Well, Angie, it looks as if you'd found your job right here at home, doesn't it? This young lady's just one of hundreds, I suppose. Thousands. You can have the whole house for them, if you want it, Angie, and the grounds, and all the money you need. I guess we've kind of overlooked the girls. Hm, Angie? What d'you say?"

But Tessie was not listening. She had scarcely heard. Her face was white with earnestness.

"Can you speak French?"

"Yes," Angie answered.

"Well," said Tessie, and gulped once, "well, how do you say in French: 'Give me a piece of bread'? That's what I want to learn first."

Angie Hatton said it correctly.

"That's it! Wait a minute! Say it again, will you?"

Angie said it again, Tessie wet her lips. Her cheeks were smeared with tears and dirt. Her hair was wild and her blouse awry. *"Donnay-ma-un-morso-doo-pang,"* she articulated painfully. And in that moment, as she put her hand in that of Chuck Mory, across the ocean, her face was very beautiful with contentment.

Long Distance

Chet Ball was painting a wooden chicken yellow. The wooden chicken was mounted on a six-by-twelve board. The board was mounted on four tiny wheels. The whole would eventually be pulled on a string guided by the plump, moist hand of some blissful five-year-old.

You got the incongruity of it the instant your eye fell upon Chet Ball. Chet's shoulders alone would have loomed large in contrast with any wooden toy ever devised, including the Trojan horse. Everything about him, from the big, blunt-fingered hands that held the ridiculous chick to the great muscular pillar of his neck, was in direct opposition to his task, his surroundings, and his attitude.

Chet's proper milieu was Chicago, Illinois (the West Side); his job that of lineman for the Gas, Light & Power Company; his normal working position astride the top of a telegraph pole, supported in his perilous perch by a lineman's leather belt and the kindly fates, both of which are likely to trick you in an emergency.

Yet now he lolled back among his pillows, dabbing complacently at the absurd yellow toy. A description of his surroundings would sound like pages 3 to 17 of a novel by Mrs. Humphry Ward. The place was all greensward, and terraces, and sundials, and beeches, and even those rhododendrons without which no English novel or country estate is complete. The presence of Chet Ball among his pillows and some hundreds similarly disposed revealed to you at once the fact that this particular English estate was now transformed into Reconstruction Hospital No. 9.

The painting of the chicken quite finished (including two beady black paint eyes), Chet was momentarily at a loss. Miss Kate had not told him to stop painting when the chicken was completed. Miss Kate was at the other end of the sunny garden walk, bending over a wheel chair. So Chet went on painting, placidly. One by one, with meticulous nicety, he painted all his fingernails a bright and cheery yellow. Then he did the whole of his left thumb and was starting on the second joint of the index finger when Miss Kate came up behind him and took the brush gently from his strong hands.

"You shouldn't have painted your fingers," she said.

Chet surveyed them with pride. "They look swell."

Miss Kate did not argue the point. She put the freshly painted wooden chicken on the table to dry in the sun. Her eyes fell upon a letter bearing an American postmark and addressed to Sergeant Chester Ball, with a lot of cryptic figures and letters strung out after it, such as A.E.F. and Co. 11.

"Here's a letter for you!" She infused a lot of Glad into her voice. But Chet only cast a languid eye upon it and said, "Yeh?"

"I'll read it to you, shall I? It's a nice fat one."

Chet sat back, indifferent, negatively acquiescent. And Miss Kate began to read in her clear young voice, there in the sunshine and scent of the centuries-old

English garden.

It marked an epoch in Chet's life — that letter. It reached out across the Atlantic Ocean from the Chester Ball of his Chicago days, before he had even heard of English gardens.

Your true lineman has a daredevil way with the women, as have all men whose calling is a hazardous one. Chet was a crack workman. He could shinny up a pole, strap his emergency belt, open his tool kit, wield his pliers with expert deftness, and climb down again in record time. It was his pleasure — and seemingly the pleasure and privilege of all lineman's gangs the world over — to whistle blithely and to call impudently to any passing petticoat that caught his fancy.

Perched three feet from the top of the high pole he would cling protected, seemingly, by some force working in direct defiance of the law of gravity. And now and then, by way of brightening the tedium of their job, he and his gang would call to a girl passing in the street below, "Hoo-hoo! Hello, sweetheart!"

There was nothing vicious in it. Chet would have come to the aid of beauty in distress as quickly as Don Quixote. Any man with a blue shirt as clean and a shave as smooth and a haircut as round as Chet Ball's has no meanness in him. A certain daredevilry went hand in hand with his work — a calling in which a careless load dispatcher, a cut wire, or a faulty strap may mean instant death. Usually the girls laughed and called back to them or went on more quickly, the color in their cheeks a little higher.

But not Anastasia Rourke. Early the first morning of a two-week job on the new plant of the Western Castings Company, Chet Ball, glancing down from his dizzy perch atop an electric-light pole, espied Miss Anastasia Rourke going to work. He didn't know her name or anything about her, except that she was pretty.

You could see that from a distance even more remote than Chet's. But you couldn't know that Stasia was a lady not to be trifled with. We know her name was Rourke, but he didn't.

So then: "Hoo-hoo!" he had called. "Hello, sweetheart! Wait for me and I'll be down."

Stasia Rourke had lifted her face to where he perched so high above the streets. Her cheeks were five shades pinker than was their wont, which would make them border on the red.

"You big ape, you!" she called, in her clear, crisp voice. "If you had your foot on the ground you wouldn't dast call to a decent girl like that. If you were down here I'd slap the face of you. You know you're safe up there."

The words were scarcely out of her mouth before Chet Ball's sturdy legs were twinkling down the pole. His spurred heels dug into the soft pine of the pole with little ripe, tearing sounds. He walked up to Stasia and stood squarely in front of her, six feet of brawn and brazen nerve. One ruddy cheek he presented to her astonished gaze. "Hello, sweetheart," he said. And waited. The Rourke girl hesitated just a second. All the Irish heart in her was melting at the boyish impudence of the man before her. Then she lifted one hand and slapped his smooth cheek. It was a ringing slap. You saw the four marks of her fingers upon his face. Chet straightened, his blue eyes bluer. Stasia looked up at him, her eyes wide. Then down at her own hand, as if it belonged to somebody else. Her hand came up to her own face. She burst into tears, turned, and ran. And as she ran, and as she wept, she saw that Chet was still standing there, looking after her.

Next morning, when Stasia Rourke went by to work, Chet Ball was standing at the foot of the pole, waiting.

They were to have been married that next June. But

that next June Chet Ball, perched perilously on the branch of a tree in a small woodsy spot somewhere in France, was one reason why the American artillery in that same woodsy spot was getting such a deadly range on the enemy. Chet's costume was so devised that even through field glasses (made in Germany) you couldn't tell where tree left off and Chet began.

Then, quite suddenly, the Germans got the range. The tree in which Chet was hidden came down with a crash, and Chet lay there, more than ever indiscernible among its tender foliage.

Which brings us back to the English garden, the yellow chicken, Miss Kate, and the letter.

His shattered leg was mended by one of those miracles of modern war surgery, though he never again would dig his spurred heels into the pine of a G. L. & P. Company pole. But the other thing — they put it down under the broad general head of shock. In the lovely English garden they set him to weaving and painting as a means of soothing the shattered nerves. He had made everything from pottery jars to bead chains, from baskets to rugs. Slowly the tortured nerves healed. But the doctors, when they stopped at Chet's cot or chair, talked always of "the memory center." Chet seemed satisfied to go on placidly painting toys or weaving chains with his great, square-tipped fingers — the fingers that had wielded the pliers so cleverly in his pole-climbing days.

"It's just something that only luck or an accident can mend," said the nerve specialist. "Time may do it — but I doubt it. Sometimes just a word — the right word — will set the thing in motion again. Does he get any letters?"

"His girl writes to him. Fine letters. But she doesn't know yet about — about this. I've written his letters for him. She knows now that his leg is healed and she wonders —"

That had been a month ago. Today Miss Kate slit the envelope post-marked Chicago. Chet was fingering the yellow wooden chicken, pride in his eyes. In Miss Kate's eyes there was a troubled, baffled look as she began to read:

> Chet, dear, it's raining in Chicago. And you know when it rains in Chicago it's wetter, and muddier, and rainier than anyplace in the world. Except maybe this Flanders we're reading so much about. They say for rain and mud that place takes the prize.
>
> I don't know what I'm going on about rain and mud for, Chet darling, when it's you I'm thinking of. Nothing else and nobody else. Chet, I got a funny feeling there's something you're keeping back from me. You're hurt worse than just the leg. Boy, dear, don't you know it won't make any difference with me how you look, or feel, or anything? I don't care how bad you're smashed up. I'd rather have you without any features at all than any other man with two sets. Whatever's happened to the outside of you, they can't change your insides. And you're the same man that called out to me that day, "Hoo-hoo! Hello, sweetheart!" and when I gave you a piece of my mind, climbed down off the pole, and put your face up to be slapped, God bless the boy in you —

A sharp little sound from him. Miss Kate looked up, quickly. Chet Ball was staring at the beady-eyed yellow chicken in his hand.

"What's this thing?" he demanded in a strange voice.

Miss Kate answered him very quietly, trying to keep her own voice easy and natural. "That's a toy chicken, cut out of wood."

"What'm I doin' with it?"

"You've just finished painting it."

Chet Ball held it in his great hand and stared at it for a brief moment, struggling between anger and amusement. And between anger and amusement he put it down on the table none too gently and stood up, yawning a little.

"That's a hell of a job for a he-man!" Then in utter contrition: "Oh, beggin' your pardon! That was fierce! I didn't —"

But there was nothing shocked about the expression on Miss Kate's face. She was registering joy — pure joy.

The Maternal Feminine

Called upon to describe Aunt Sophy, you would have to coin a term or fall back on the dictionary definition of a spinster. "An unmarried woman," states that worthy work, baldly, "especially when no longer young." That, to the world, was Sophy Decker. Unmarried, certainly. And most certainly no longer young. In figure, she was, at fifty, what is known in the corset ads as a "stylish stout." Well dressed in dark suits, with broad-toed health shoes and a small, astute hat. The suit was practical common sense. The health shoes were comfort. The hat was strictly business. Sophy Decker made and sold hats, both astute and ingenuous, to the female population of Chippewa, Wisconsin. Chippewa's East End set bought the knowing type of hat, and the mill hands and hired girls bought the naïve ones. But whether lumpy or possessed of that thing known as line, Sophy Decker's hats were honest hats.

The world is full of Aunt Sophys, unsung. Plump, ruddy, capable women of middle age. Unwed, and rather looked down upon by a family of married sisters and tolerant, good-humored brothers-in-law, and careless nieces and nephews.

"Poor Aunt Soph," with a significant half smile. "She's such a good old thing. And she's had so little in life, really."

She was, undoubtedly, a good old thing — Aunt Soph. Forever sending a model hat to this pert little niece in Seattle; or taking Adele, Sister Flora's daughter, to Chicago or New York as a treat on one of her buying trips.

Burdening herself, on her business visits to these cities, with a dozen foolish shopping commissions for the idle womenfolk of her family. Hearing without partisanship her sisters' complaints about their husbands, and her sisters' husbands' complaints about their wives. It was always the same.

"I'm telling you this, Sophy. I wouldn't breathe it to another living soul. But I honestly think, sometimes, that if it weren't for the children —"

There is no knowing why they confided these things to Sophy instead of to each other, these wedded sisters of hers. Perhaps they held for each other an unuttered distrust or jealousy. Perhaps, in making a confidante of Sophy, there was something of the satisfaction that comes of dropping a surreptitious stone down a deep well and hearing it plunk, safe in the knowledge that it has struck no one and that it cannot rebound, lying there in the soft darkness. Sometimes they would end by saying, "But you don't know what it is, Sophy. You can't. I'm sure I don't know why I'm telling you all this."

But when Sophy answered, sagely, "I know; I know," they paid little heed, once having unburdened themselves. The curious part of it is that she did know. She knew as a woman of fifty must know who, all her life, has given and given and in return has received nothing. Sophy Decker had never used the word inhibition in her life. She may not have known what it meant. She only knew (without in the least knowing she knew) that in giving of her goods, of her affections, of her time, of her energy, she found a certain relief. Her own people would have been shocked if you had told them that there was about this old-maid aunt something rather splendidly Rabelaisian. Without being what is known as a masculine woman, she had, somehow, acquired the man's viewpoint, his shrewd value sense. She ate a good deal, and enjoyed her food. She did not care for those queer little stories that married women sometimes tell, with narrowed eyes, but she was strangely tolerant of what is known as sin. So simple and direct she was that you wondered how she prospered in a line so subtle as the millinery business.

You might have got a fairly true characterization of Sophy Decker from one of fifty people: from a salesman in a New York or Chicago wholesale millinery house; from Otis Cowan, cashier of the First National Bank of Chippewa; from Julia Gold, her head milliner and trimmer; from almost anyone, in fact, except a member of her own family. They knew her least of all. Her three married sisters — Grace in Seattle, Ella in Chicago, and Flora in Chippewa — regarded her with a rather affectionate disapproval from the snug safety of their own conjugal inglenooks.

"I don't know. There's something — well — common about Sophy," Flora confided to Ella. Flora, on shopping bent, and Sophy, seeking hats, had made the five-hour run from Chippewa to Chicago together. "She talks to everybody. You should have heard her with the porter on our train. Chums! And when the conductor took our tickets it was a social occasion. You know how packed the seven-fifty-two is. Every seat in the parlor car taken. And Sophy asking the colored porter about how his wife was getting along — she called him William — and if they were going to send her West, and all about her. I wish she wouldn't."

*A*unt Sophy undeniably had a habit of regarding people as human beings. You found her talking to chambermaids and delivery boys, and elevator starters, and gas collectors, and hotel clerks — all that aloof, unapproachable, superior crew. Under her benign volubility they bloomed and spread and took on color as do those tight little paper water flowers when you cast them into a bowl. It wasn't idle curiosity in her. She was interested. You found yourself confiding to her your innermost longings, your secret tribulations, under the encouragement of her sympathetic, "You don't say!" Perhaps it was as well that Sister Flora was in ignorance of the fact that the millinery salesmen at Danowitz & Danowitz, Importers, always called Miss Decker Aunt Soph, as, with one arm flung about her plump shoulder, they revealed to her the picture of their girl in the back flap of their billfold.

Flora, with a firm grip on Chippewa society, as represented by the East End set, did not find her position enhanced by a sister in the millinery business in Elm Street.

"Of course it's wonderful that she's self-supporting and successful and all," she told her husband. "But it's not so pleasant for Adele, now that she's growing up, having all the girls she knows buying their hats of her aunt. Not that I — but you know how it is."

H. Charnsworth Baldwin said yes, he knew.

When the Decker girls were young, the Deckers had lived in a sagging old frame house (from which the original paint had long ago peeled in great scrofulous patches) on an unimportant street in Chippewa. There was a worm-eaten, russet-apple tree in the yard, an untidy tangle of wild-cucumber vine over the front porch, and an uncut brush of sunburned grass and weeds all about.

From May until September you never passed the Decker place without hearing the plunkety-plink of a mandolin from somewhere behind the vines, laughter, and the creak-creak of the hard-worked and protesting hammock hooks.

Flora, Ella, and Grace Decker had had more beaux and fewer clothes than any other girls in Chippewa. In a town full of pretty young things, they were, undoubtedly, the prettiest; and in a family of pretty sisters (Sophy always excepted) Flora was the acknowledged beauty. She was the kind of girl whose nose never turns red on a frosty morning. A little, white, exquisite nose, purest example of the degree of perfection which may be attained by that vulgarest of features. Under her great gray eyes were faint violet shadows which gave her a look of almost poignant wistfulness. Her slow, sweet smile give the beholder an actual physical pang. Only her family knew she was lazy as a behemoth, untidy about her person, and as sentimental as a hungry shark. The strange and cruel part of it was that, in some grotesque, exaggerated way, as a cartoon may be like a photograph, Sophy resembled Flora. It was as though nature, in prankish mood, had given a cabbage the color and texture of a rose, with none of its fragile reticence and grace.

It was a manless household. Mrs. Decker, vague, garrulous, referred to her dead husband, in frequent reminiscence, as poor Mr. Decker. Mrs. Decker dragged one leg as she walked — rheumatism, or a spinal affection. Small wonder, then, that Sophy, the plain, with a gift for hatmaking, a knack at eggless cake baking, and a genius for turning a sleeve so that last year's style met this year's without a struggle, contributed nothing to the sag in the center of the old twine hammock on the front porch.

That the three girls should marry well, and Sophy not at all, was as inevitable as the sequence of the seasons. Ella and Grace did not manage badly, considering that they had only their girlish prettiness and the twine hammock to work with. But Flora, with her beauty, captured H. Charnsworth Baldwin. Chippewa gasped. H. Charnsworth Baldwin drove a skittish mare to a high-wheeled yellow runabout; had his clothes made at Proctor Brothers in Milwaukee; and talked about a game called golf. It was he who advocated laying out a section of land for what he called links, and erecting a clubhouse thereon.

"The section of the bluff overlooking the river," he explained, "is full of natural hazards, besides having a really fine view."

Chippewa — or that comfortable, middle-class section of it which got its exercise walking home to dinner from the store at noon, and cutting the grass evenings after supper — laughed as it read this interview in the Chippewa Eagle.

"A golf course," they repeated to one another, grinning. "Conklin's cow pasture, up the river. It's full of natural — wait a minute — what was? — oh, yeh, here it is — hazards. Full of natural hazards. Say, couldn't you die!"

For H. Charnsworth Baldwin had been little Henry Baldwin before he went East to college. Ten years later H. Charnsworth, in knickerbockers and gay-topped stockings, was winning the cup in the men's tournament played on the Chippewa golf-club course, overlooking the river. And his name, in stout gold letters, blinked at you from the plate-glass windows of the office at the corner of Elm and Winnebago:

NORTHERN LUMBER AND LAND COMPANY
H. CHARNSWORTH BALDWIN, PRES.

Two blocks farther down Elm Street was another sign, not so glittering, which read:

MISS SOPHY DECKER
MILLINERY

Sophy's hatmaking, in the beginning, had been done at home. She had always made her sisters' hats, and her own, of course, and an occasional hat for a girl friend. After her sisters had married, Sophy found herself in possession of a rather bewildering amount of spare time. The hat trade grew so that sometimes there were six rather botchy little bonnets all done up in yellow paper pyramids with a pin at the top, awaiting their future wearers. After her mother's death Sophy still stayed on in the old house. She took a course in millinery in Milwaukee, came home, stuck up a home-made sign in the parlor window (the untidy cucumber vines came down), and began her hatmaking in earnest. In five years she had opened a shop on a side street near Elm, had painted the old house, installed new plumbing, built a warty stucco porch, and transformed the weedy, grass-tangled yard into an orderly stretch of green lawn and bright flower beds. In ten years she was in Elm Street, and the Chippewa Eagle ran a half column twice a year describing her spring and fall openings. On these occasions Aunt Sophy, in black satin and marcel wave and her most relentless corsets, was, in all the superficial things, not a pleat or fold or line or wave behind her city colleagues. She had all the catch phrases:

"This is awfully good this year."

"Here's a sweet thing. A Mornet model."

". . . Well, but, my dear, it's the style — the line — you're paying for, not the material."

"No, that hat doesn't do a thing for you."

"I've got it. I had you in mind when I bought it. Now don't say you can't wear henna. Wait till you see it on."

When she stood behind you as you sat, uncrowned and expectant before the mirror, she would poise the hat four inches above your head, holding it in the tips of her fingers, a precious, fragile thing. Your fascinated eyes were held by it, and your breath as well. Then down it descended, slowly, slowly. A quick pressure.

Her fingers firm against your temples. A little sigh of relieved suspense.

"That's wonderful on you! . . . You don't! Oh, my dear! But that's because you're not used to it. You know how you said, for years, you had to have a brim, and couldn't possibly wear a turban, with your nose, until I proved to you that if the head size was only big . . . Well, perhaps this needs just a lit-tle lift here. Ju-u-ust a nip. There! That does it."

And that did it. Not that Sophy Decker ever tried to sell you a hat against your judgment, taste, or will. She was too wise a psychologist and too shrewd a business-woman for that. She preferred that you go out of her shop hatless rather than with an unbecoming hat. But whether you bought or not you took with you out of Sophy Decker's shop something more precious than any hatbox ever contained. Just to hear her admonishing a customer, her good-natured face all aglow:

"My dear, always put on your hat before you get into your dress.

I do. You can get your arms above your head, and set it right. I put on my hat and veil as soon's I get my hair combed."

In your mind's eye you saw her, a stout, well-stayed

figure in tight brassiere and scant slip, bare-armed and bare-bosomed, in smart hat and veil, attired as though for the street from the neck up and for the bedroom from the shoulders down.

The East End set bought Sophy Decker's hats because they were modish and expensive hats. But she managed, miraculously, to gain a large and lucrative following among the paper-mill girls and factory hands as well. You would have thought that any attempt to hold both these opposites would cause her to lose one or the other. Aunt Sophy said, frankly, that of the two, she would have preferred to lose her smart trade.

"The mill girls come in with their money in their hands, you might say. They get good wages and they want to spend them. I wouldn't try to sell them one of those little plain model hats. They wouldn't understand 'em or like them. And if I told them the price they'd think I was trying to cheat them. They want a hat with something good and solid on it. Their fathers wouldn't prefer caviar to pork roast, would they? It's the same idea."

Her shop windows reflected her business acumen. One was chastely, severely elegant, holding a single hat poised on a slender stick.

In the other were a dozen honest arrangements of velvet and satin and plumes.

At the spring opening she always displayed one of those little toques completely covered with violets. That violet-covered toque was a symbol.

"I don't expect 'em to buy it," Sophy Decker explained. "But everybody feels there should be a hat like that at a spring opening. It's like a fruit centerpiece at a family dinner. Nobody ever eats it, but it has to be there."

The two Baldwin children — Adele and Eugene —

found Aunt Sophy's shop a treasure trove. Adele, during her doll days, possessed such boxes of satin and velvet scraps, and bits of lace and ribbon and jet as to make her the envy of all her playmates. She used to crawl about the floor of the shop workroom and under the table and chairs like a little scavenger.

"What in the world do you do with all that truck, child?" asked Aunt Sophy. "You must have barrels of it."

Adele stuffed another wisp of tulle into the pocket of her pinafore.

"I keep it," she said.

When she was ten Adele had said to her mother, "Why do you always say 'Poor Sophy'?"

"Because — Aunt Sophy's had so little in life. She never has married, and has always worked."

Adele considered that. "If you don't get married do they say you're poor?"

"Well — yes —"

"Then I'll get married," announced Adele. A small, dark, eerie child, skinny and rather foreign-looking. The boy, Eugene, had the beauty which should have been the girl's. Very tall, very blond, with the straight nose and wistful eyes of the Flora of twenty years ago. "If only Adele could have had his looks," his mother used to say. "They're wasted on a man. He doesn't need them, but a girl does. Adele will have to be well dressed and interesting. And that's such hard work."

Flora said she worshiped her children. And she actually sometimes still coquetted heavily with her husband. At twenty she had been addicted to baby talk when endeavoring to coax something out of someone. Her admirers had found it irresistible. At forty it was awful. Her selfishness was colossal. She affected a semi-invalidism and for fifteen years had spent one day a week in bed. She took no exercise and a great deal of soda bicarbonate and tried to fight her fat with baths. Fifteen or twenty years had worked a startling change in the two sisters, Flora the beautiful and Sophy the plain. It was more than a mere physical change. It was a spiritual thing, though neither knew nor marked it. Each had taken on weight, the one, solidly, comfortably; the other, flabbily, unhealthily. With the encroaching fat, Flora's small, delicate features seemed, somehow, to disappear in her face, so that you saw it as a large white surface bearing indentations, ridges, and hollows like one of those enlarged photographs of the moon's surface as seen through a telescope. A self-centered face, and misleadingly placid. Aunt Sophy's large, plain features, plumply padded now, impressed you as indicating strength, courage, and a great human understanding.

From her husband and her children, Flora exacted service that would have chafed a galley slave into rebellion. She loved to lie in bed, in an orchid bed jacket with ribbons, and be read to by Adele, or Eugene, or her husband. They all hated it.

"She just wants to be waited on, and petted, and admired," Adele had stormed one day, in open rebellion, to her Aunt Sophy. "She uses it as an excuse for everything and has, ever since Gene and I were children. She's as strong as an ox." Not a daughterly speech, but true.

Years before, a generous but misguided woman friend, coming in to call, had been ushered in to where Mrs. Baldwin lay propped up in a nest of pillows.

"Well, I don't blame you," the caller had gushed. "If I looked the way you do in bed I'd stay there forever. Don't tell me you're sick, with all that lovely color!"

Flora Baldwin had rolled her eyes ceilingward. "Nobody ever gives me credit for all my suffering and ill-health. And just because all my blood is in my cheeks."

Flora was ambitious, socially, but too lazy to make the effort necessary for success in that direction.

"I love my family," she would say. "They fill my life. After all, that's a profession in itself — being a wife and mother."

She showed her devotion by taking no interest whatever in her husband's land schemes; by forbidding Eugene to play football at school for fear he might be injured; by impressing Adele with the necessity for vivacity and modishness because of what she called her unfortunate lack of beauty.

"I don't understand it," she used to say in the child's presence. "Her father's handsome enough, goodness knows; and I wasn't such a fright when I was a girl. And look at her! Little dark skinny thing."

The boy, Eugene, grew up a very silent, handsome, shy young fellow. The girl, dark, voluble, and rather interesting. The husband, more and more immersed in his business, was absent from home for long periods irritable after some of these home-comings; boisterously high-spirited following other trips. Now growling about household expenses and unpaid bills; now urging the purchase of some almost prohibitive luxury. Anyone but a nagging, self-absorbed, and vain woman such as Flora would have marked these unmistakable signs. But Flora was a taker, not a giver. She thought herself affectionate because she craved affection unduly. She thought herself a fond mother because she insisted on having her children with her, under her thumb, marking their devotion as a prisoner marks time with his feet, stupidly, shufflingly, advancing not a step.

Sometimes Sophy, the clear-eyed, seeing this state of affairs, tried to stop it.

"You expect too much of your husband and children," she said one day, bluntly, to her sister.

"I!" Flora's dimpled hand had flown to her breast like a wounded thing. "I! You're crazy! There isn't a more devoted wife and mother in the world. That's the trouble. I love them too much."

"Well, then," grimly, "stop it for a change. That's half Eugene's nervousness — your fussing over him. He's eighteen. Give him a chance. You're weakening him. And stop dinning that society stuff into Adele's ears. She's got brains, that child. Why, just yesterday, in the workroom, she got hold of some satin and a shape and turned out a little turban that Angie Hatton —"

"Do you mean to tell me that Angie Hatton saw my Adele working in your shop! Now, look here, Sophy. You're earning your living, and it's to your credit. You're my sister. But I won't have Adele associated in the minds of my friends with your hat store, understand? I won't have it. That isn't what I sent her away to an expensive school for. To have her come back and sit around a millinery workshop with a lot of little, cheap, shoddy sewing girls! Now, understand, I won't have it! You don't know what it is to be a mother. You don't know what it is to have suffered. If you had brought two children into the world —"

So, then, it had come about during the years between their childhood and their youth that Aunt Sophy received the burden of their confidences, their griefs, their perplexities. She seemed, somehow, to understand in some miraculous way, and to make the burden a welcome one.

"Well, now, you tell Aunt Sophy all about it. Stop crying, Della. How can I hear when you're crying! That's my baby. Now, then."

This when they were children. But with the years the habit clung and became fixed. There was something about Aunt Sophy's house — the old frame house with the warty stucco porch. For that matter, there was something about the very shop downtown, with its workroom in the rear, that had a cozy, homelike quality never possessed by the big Baldwin house. H. Charnsworth Baldwin had built a large brick mansion, in the Tudor style, on a bluff overlooking the Fox River, in the best residential section of Chippewa. It was expensively furnished. The hall console alone was enough to strike a preliminary chill to your heart.

The millinery workroom, winter days, was always bright and warm and snug. The air was a little close, perhaps, and heavy, but with a not unpleasant smell of dyes and stuffs and velvet and glue and steam and flatiron and a certain racy scent that Julia Gold, the head trimmer, always used. There was a sociable cat, white with a dark-gray patch on his throat and a swipe of it across one flank that spoiled him for style and beauty but made him a comfortable-looking cat to have around. Sometimes, on very cold days, or in the rush season, the girls would not go home to dinner, but would bring their lunches and cook coffee over a little gas heater in the corner. Julia Gold, especially, drank quantities of coffee. Aunt Sophy had hired her from Chicago. She had been with her for five years. She said Julia was the best trimmer she had ever had. Aunt Sophy often took her to New York or Chicago on her buying trips. Julia had not much genius for original design, or she never would have been content to be head milliner in a small-town shop. But she could copy a fifty-dollar model from memory down to the last detail of crown and brim. It was a gift that made her invaluable.

The boy, Eugene, used to like to look at Julia Gold. Her hair was very black and her face was very white, and her eyebrows met in a thick dark line. Her face as

she bent over her work was sullen and brooding, but
when she lifted her head suddenly, in conversation,
you were startled by a vivid flash of teeth and eyes and
smile. Her voice was deep and low. She made you a
little uncomfortable. Her eyes seemed always to be
asking something. Around the worktable, mornings,
she used to relate the dream she had had the night
before. In these dreams she was always being pursued
by a lover. "And then I woke up, screaming." Neither
she nor the sewing girls knew what she was revealing
in these confidences of hers. But Aunt Sophy, the
shrewd, somehow sensed it.

"You're alone too much, evenings. That's what
comes of living in a boardinghouse. You come over to
me for a week. The change will do you good, and it'll
be nice for me, too, having somebody to keep me
company."

Julia often came for a week or ten days at a time.
Julia, about the house after supper, was given to those
vivid splashy negligees with big flower patterns strewn
over them. They made her hair look blacker and her
skin whiter by contrast. Sometimes Eugene or Adele
or both would drop in and the four would play bridge.
Aunt Sophy played a shrewd and canny game, Adele a
rather brilliant one, Julia a wild and disastrous hand,
always, and Eugene so badly that only Julia would take
him on as a partner. Mrs. Baldwin never knew about
these evenings.

It was on one of these occasions that Aunt Sophy,
coming unexpectedly into the living room from the
kitchen, where she and Adele were foraging for refresh-
ments after the game, beheld Julia Gold and Eugene,
arms clasped about each other, cheek to cheek. They
started up as she came in and faced her, the woman
defiantly, the boy bravely. Julia Gold was thirty (with
reservations) at that time, and the boy not quite twenty-

one.

"How long?" said Aunt Sophy, quietly. She had a mayonnaise spoon and a leaf of lettuce in her hand then, and still she did not look comic.

"I'm crazy about her," said Eugene. "We're crazy about each other. We're going to be married."

Aunt Sophy listened for the reassuring sound of Adele's spoons and plates in the kitchen. She came forward. "Now, listen —" she began.

"I love him," said Julia Gold, dramatically. "I love him!"

Except that it was very white and, somehow, old-looking, Aunt Sophy's face was as benign as always. "Now, look here, Julia, my girl. That isn't love, and you know it. I'm an old maid, but I know what love is when I see it. I'm ashamed of you, Julia. Sensible woman like you, hugging and kissing a boy like that, and old enough to be his mother."

"Now, look here, Aunt Sophy! If you're going to talk that way — Why, she's wonderful. She's taught me what it means to really —"

"Oh, my land!" Aunt Sophy sat down, looking suddenly very ill.

And then, from the kitchen, Adele's clear young voice: "Heh! What's the idea! I'm not going to do all the work. Where's everybody?"

Aunt Sophy started up again. She came up to them and put a hand — a capable, firm, steadying hand — on the arm of each. The woman drew back, but the boy did not.

"Will you promise me not to do anything for a week? Just a week! Will you promise me? Will you?"

"Are you going to tell Father?"

"Not for a week, if you'll promise not to see each other in that week. No, I don't want to send you away, Julia, I don't want to. . . . You're not a bad girl. It's just

— he's never had — at home they never gave him a chance. Just a week, Julia. Just a week, Eugene. We can talk things over then."

Adele's footsteps coming from the kitchen.

"Quick!"

"I promise," said Eugene. Julia said nothing.

"Well, really," said Adele, from the doorway, "you're a nervy lot, sitting around while I slave in the kitchen. Gene, see if you can open the olives with this fool can opener. I tried."

There is no knowing what she expected to do in that week, Aunt Sophy; what miracle she meant to perform. She had no plan in her mind. Just hope. She looked strangely shrunken and old, suddenly. But when, three days later, the news came that America was to go into the war she had her answer.

Flora was beside herself. "Eugene won't have to go. He isn't old enough, thank God! And by the time he is it will be over. Surely." She was almost hysterical.

Eugene was in the room. Aunt Sophy looked at him and he looked at Aunt Sophy. In her eyes was a question. In his was the answer. They said nothing. The next day Eugene enlisted. In three days he was gone. Flora took to her bed. Next day Adele, a faint, unwonted color marking her cheeks, walked into her mother's bedroom and stood at the side of the recumbent figure. Her father, his hands clasped behind him, was pacing up and down, now and then kicking a cushion that had fallen to the floor. He was chewing a dead cigar, one side of his face twisted curiously over the cylinder in his mouth so that he had a sinister and crafty look.

"Charnsworth, won't you please stop ramping up and down like that! My nerves are killing me. I can't help it if the war has done something or other to your business. I'm sure no wife could have been more economical than I have. Nothing matters but Eugene, anyway. How could he do such a thing! I've given my whole life to my children —"

H. Charnsworth kicked the cushion again so that it struck the wall at the opposite side of the room. Flora drew her breath in between her teeth as though a knife had entered her heart.

Adele still stood at the side of the bed, looking at her mother. Her hands were clasped behind her, too. In that moment, as she stood there, she resembled her mother and her father so startlingly and simultaneously that the two, had they been less absorbed in their own affairs, must have marked it.

The girl's head came up stiffly. "Listen. I'm going to marry Daniel Oakley."

Daniel Oakley was fifty, and a friend of her father's. For years he had been coming to the house and for years she had ridiculed him. She and Eugene had called him Sturdy Oak because he was always talking about his strength and endurance, his walks, his rugged health; pounding his chest meanwhile and planting his feet far apart. He and Baldwin had had business relations as well as friendly ones.

At this announcement Flora screamed and sat up in bed. H. Charnsworth stopped short in his pacing and regarded his daughter with a queer look; a concentrated look, as though what she had said had set in motion a whole mass of mental machinery within his brain.

"When did he ask you?"

"He's asked me a dozen times. But it's different now. All the men will be going to war. There won't be any left. Look at England and France. I'm not going to be left." She turned squarely toward her father, her young face set and hard. "You know what I mean. You know what I mean."

Flora, sitting up in bed, was sobbing. "I think you

might have told your mother, Adele. What are children coming to! You stand there and say, 'I'm going to marry Daniel Oakley.' Oh, I am so faint . . . all of a sudden . . . Get the spirits of ammonia."

Adele turned and walked out of the room. She was married six weeks later. They had a regular prewar wedding — veil, flowers, dinner, and all. Aunt Sophy arranged the folds of her gown and draped her veil. The girl stood looking at herself in the mirror, a curious half smile twisting her lips. She seemed slighter and darker than ever.

"In all this white, and my veil, I look just like a fly in a quart of milk," she said, with a laugh. Then, suddenly, she turned to her aunt, who stood behind her, and clung to her, holding her tight, tight. "I can't!" she gasped. "I can't! I can't!"

Aunt Sophy held her off and looked at her, her eyes searching the girl.

"What do you mean, Della? Are you just nervous or do you mean you don't want to marry him? Do you mean that? Then what are you marrying for? Tell me! Tell your Aunt Sophy."

But Adele was straightening herself and pulling out the crushed folds of her veil. "To pay the mortgage on the old homestead, of course. Just like the girl in the play." She laughed a little. But Aunt Sophy did not.

"Now look here, Della. If you're —"

But there was a knock at the door. Adele caught up her flowers. "It's all right," she said. Aunt Sophy stood with her back against the door. "If it's money," she said. "It is! It is, isn't it! I've got money saved. It was for you children. I've always been afraid. I knew he was sailing pretty close, with his speculations and all, since the war. He can have it all. It isn't too late yet. Adele! Della, my baby."

"Don't, Aunt Sophy. It wouldn't be enough, anyway.

Daniel has been wonderful, really. Dad's been stealing money for years. Dan's. Don't look like that. I'd have hated being poor, anyway.

Never could have got used to it. It is ridiculous, though, isn't it? Like something in the movies. I don't mind. I'm lucky, really, when you come to think of it. A plain little black thing like me."

"But your mother —"

"Mother doesn't know a thing."

Flora wept mistily all through the ceremony, but Adele was composed enough for two.

When, scarcely a month later, Baldwin came to Sophy Decker, his face drawn and queer, Sophy knew.

"How much?" she said.

"Thirty thousand will cover it. If you've got more than that —"

"I thought Oakley — Adele said —"

"He did, but he won't anymore, and this thing's got to be met. It's this damned war that's done it. I'd have been all right. People got scared. They wanted their money. They wanted it in cash."

"Speculating with it, were you?"

"Oh, well, a woman doesn't understand these business deals."

"No, naturally," said Aunt Sophy, "a butterfly like me."

"Sophy, for God's sake don't joke now. I tell you this will cover it, and everything will be all right. If I had anybody else to go to for the money I wouldn't ask you. But you'll get it back. You know that."

Aunt Sophy got up, heavily, and went over to her desk. "It was for the children, anyway. They won't need it now."

He looked up at that. Something in her voice. "Who won't? Why won't they?"

"I don't know what made me say that. I had a

dream."

"Eugene?"

"Yes."

"Oh, well, we're all nervous. Flora has dreams every night and presentiments every fifteen minutes. Now, look here, Sophy. About this money. You'll never know how grateful I am. Flora doesn't understand these things, but I can talk to you. It's like this —"

"I might as well be honest about it," Sophy interrupted. "I'm doing it, not for you, but for Flora, and Della — and Eugene. Flora has lived such a sheltered life. I sometimes wonder if she ever really knew any of you. Her husband, or her children. I sometimes have the feeling that Della and Eugene are my children — were my children."

When he came home that night Baldwin told his wife that old Soph was getting queer. "She talks about the children being hers," he said.

"Oh, well, she's awfully fond of them," Flora explained. "And she's lived her little, narrow life, with nothing to bother her but her hats and her house. She doesn't know what it means to suffer as a mother suffers — poor Sophy."

"Um," Baldwin grunted.

When the official notification of Eugene's death came from the War Department, Aunt Sophy was so calm it might have appeared that Flora had been right. She took to her bed now in earnest, did Flora. Sophy neglected everything to give comfort to the stricken two.

"How can you sit there like that!" Flora would rail. "How can you sit there like that! Even if you weren't his mother, surely you must feel something."

"It's the way he died that comforts me," said Aunt Sophy.

"What difference does that make!"

AMERICAN RED CROSS
(Croix Rouge Americaine)

MY DEAR MRS. BALDWIN:

I am sure you must have been officially notified by the U.S. War Dept. of the death of your son, Lieut. Eugene H. Baldwin. But I want to write you what I can of his last hours. I was with him much of that time as his nurse. I'm sure it must mean much to a mother to hear from a woman who was privileged to be with her boy at the last.

Your son was brought to our hospital one night badly gassed from the fighting in the Argonne Forest. Ordinarily we do not receive gassed patients, as they are sent to a special hospital near here. But two nights before, the Germans wrecked that hospital, so many gassed patients have come to us.

Your son was put in the officers' ward, where the doctors who examined him told me there was absolutely no hope for him, as he had inhaled so much gas that it was only a matter of a few hours. I could scarcely believe that a man so big and strong as he was could not pull through.

The first bad attack he had, losing his breath and nearly choking, rather frightened him, although the doctor and I were both with him. He held my hand tightly in his, begging me not to leave him, and repeating, over and over, that it was good to have a woman near. He was propped high in bed and put his head on my shoulder while I fanned him until he breathed more easily. I stayed with him all that night, though I was not on duty. You see, his eyes also were badly burned. But before he died he was able to see very well. I stayed with him every minute of that night and have never seen a finer character than he showed during all that fight for life.

He had several bad attacks that night and came through each one simply because of his great will power and fighting spirit. After each attack he would grip my hand and say, "Well, we made it that time, didn't we, nurse?" Toward morning he asked me if he was going to die. I could not tell him the truth. He needed all his strength. I told him he had one chance in a thousand. He seemed to become very strong then, and sitting bolt upright in bed, he said: "Then I'll fight for it!" We kept him alive for three days, and actually thought we had won when on the third day . . .

But even in your sorrow you must be very proud to have been the mother of such a son. . . .

I am a Wisconsin girl — Madison. When this is over and I come home, will you let me see you so that I may tell you more than I can possibly write?

MARIAN KING

It was in March, six months later, that Marian King came. They had hoped for it, but never expected it. And she came. Four people were waiting in the living room of the big Baldwin house overlooking the river. Flora and her husband, Adele and Aunt Sophy. They sat, waiting. Now and then Adele would rise, nervously, and go to the window that faced the street. Flora was weeping with audible sniffs. Baldwin sat in his chair, frowning a little, a dead cigar in one corner of his mouth. Only Aunt Sophy sat quietly, waiting.

There was little conversation. None in the last five minutes. Flora broke the silence, dabbing at her face with her handkerchief as she spoke.

"Sophy, how can you sit there like that? Not that I don't envy you. I do. I remember I used to feel sorry for you. I used to say 'Poor Sophy.' But you unmarried ones are the happiest, after all. It's the married woman who drinks the cup to the last, bitter drop. There you sit, Sophy, fifty years old, and life hasn't even touched you. You don't know how cruel life can be to a mother."

Suddenly, "There!" said Adele. The other three in the room stood up and faced the door. The sound of a motor stopping outside. Daniel Oakley's hearty voice: "Well, it only took us five minutes from the station. Pretty good."

Footsteps down the hall. Marian King stood in the doorway. They faced her, the four — Baldwin and Adele and Flora and Sophy. Marian King stood a moment, uncertainly, her eyes upon them. She looked at the two older women with swift, appraising glances. Then she came into the room, quickly, and put her two hands on Aunt Soph's shoulders and looked into her eyes straight and sure.

"You must be a very proud woman," she said. "You ought to be a very proud woman."